the
Secret Passage

With faith and belief in God
and hard work you can make
all your dreams come true.

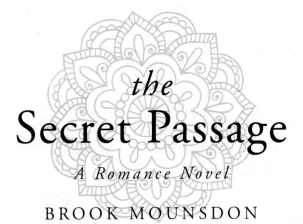

the
Secret Passage

A Romance Novel

BROOK MOUNSDON

Tate Publishing & Enterprises

Published by Tate Publishing & Enterprises, LLC
127 E. Trade Center Terrace | Mustang, Oklahoma 73064 USA
1.888.361.9473 | www.tatepublishing.com

Tate Publishing is committed to excellence in the publishing industry. The company reflects the philosophy established by the founders, based on Psalm 68:11,
"The Lord gave the word and great was the company of those who published it."

Book design copyright © 2010 by Tate Publishing, LLC. All rights reserved.
Cover design by Amber Gulilat
Interior design by Jeff Fisher

Published in the United States of America

ISBN: 978-1-61663-928-0
1. Fiction, Romance, Contemporary
2. Fiction, Romance, General
10.08.30

Dedication

I dedicate this story to my family, who pushed when I got stuck; encouraged me to not give up; put my spirits up when something would not work the way I wanted it to; and helped give me ideas through the process. I love you all.

Chapter 1

In my accident four years ago, I lost all use of my legs; the doctors said I would not regain the use of my legs, but I didn't believe them. With a lot of tough work, I am now able to walk again.

The main goal that got me through all the tough work was that I wanted to make my late husband proud of me by riding Sarge. Another goal I have is to get back into the modeling world. But I don't think that goal will ever come true again. Mom and I moved to Evansville, Minnesota. It's easier for me to get around and not be discovered.

"Alice, are you in here?"

"Mom, I'm in my room."

"What are you doing in here?"

"I'm twenty-nine. You don't need to know what I'm doing every five minutes."

"I do when your supper is done."

"Will you help me get up?"

"Keith, what's on your mind? You're playing ball like a girl!" James called.

"Just thinking about the kids."

Keith Trevor is twenty-nine and has two kids, Jane, age eight, and Caroline, age ten.

"What about them? I'm sure they're fine with their babysitter."

"No, that's not what I mean. I mean I was thinking about where I should send the kids to school."

We just moved to Evansville after my wife, Tyra, was killed by a drunk driver.

"Well, that's easy; send them to Evansville School."

"Yes, but Tyra always said that our children would go to a private school."

"I don't know what to tell you, man. Let's play some basketball. You're a little rusty."

"That's what happens when you haven't played for eight years. I've missed the competition."

My beeper went off. "I have to go. There's a fire at an apartment building, and I'm on call tonight. Bye."

"See you at choir practice."

"I'm not going to make it. Can't get a babysitter!" I yelled over my shoulder.

"Man, you need to get a wife."

"I had one, remember!"

"Thanks, Mom. Supper was great."

"You're welcome. Do you want to run into town with me, or are you too tired?"

"No, I'm fine. Let's go."

We live five miles out of town on a one-hundred-and-fifty-acre farm.

"Mom, do you hear all the sirens?"

"Yes. Maybe we'll see what they are all about."

"Will you drop me off at Rebecca's apartment? I forgot something there this afternoon."

"Sure."

We got to Rebecca's apartment and found what we were wondering about—the sirens. I jumped out of the car and started looking for Rebecca. I could not find her. I found a firefighter and asked if anybody was hurt.

"One person was hurt."

"Do you know who it is?"

"No, but we found her in apartment one-fifteen."

"Did you just say apartment one-fifteen?"

"Yes, do you know her?"

"Yes, her name is Rebecca Liebmann."

"That's good to know."

"Bye. I'm going to the hospital if you have any questions I need to answer about Rebecca."

After we got the fire calmed down I saw James and walked over to him.

"How long have you been here?" I asked.

"I followed you here."

"Did you see that girl that walked up to me?"

"Yes, what was her name?"

"I don't know. All I know is that she knew the girl who was hurt in the fire."

"You didn't get her name."

"No, why would I?"

"She looked like a model.'

"So what? She was hot."

"So you admit you can still see women."

"Shut up and go home."

"Where are you going?"

"To the hospital."

"You're going to check out that hot chick again."

"No, for your information, I'm going to the hospital to check on the girl who was hurt in the fire."

I drove five blocks to get to the hospital, irritated at James. I found out she was in room number five hundred and six on the sixth floor. As the top firefighter, part of my job is to check up on the people who get hurt in the fire. I did want to see that girl again and get her name, but I'd never tell James that.

I was daydreaming about that firefighter, about how brave he must be to run into fires. It was as though I dreamed him into real life right beside me. He appeared in the doorway. I didn't notice he was there until he knocked and asked if he could come in.

"How is she doing?" he asked.

"Okay, I think. They gave her a bunch of drugs that knocked her out. She has four cracked ribs, a broken wrist, and is suffering from smoke inhalation. I've been waiting for her to wake up to see how she feels."

"Are you her sister?"

"No, she doesn't have any family. I'm her best friend."

"I'm sorry. I don't think I got your name before."

"I'm sorry. My name is Alice Carlin, and yours is?"

"I'm Keith Trevor. Nice to meet you."

We shook hands, and it felt like he was sending vibrations through my hand to my heart. I don't know what to think of that. I haven't felt like that since my husband died. He did something I could never explain when I looked into his big brown eyes. His brown hair complemented his eyes.

He wore a ring on his left hand. He must be married.

Chapter 2

Alice was more beautiful than I thought. I hadn't felt like this since my wife died. Her blue eyes sparkled in the light, and her blonde hair was perfectly styled and hung down to her shoulders. James was right. She did look like a super-hot model. I glanced down at her left hand. She wore a ring.

"Well, it looks like she's going to be okay. I better get home to the kids."

"Thanks for stopping by to check on her. Your wife must be strong to let you go out near fires."

"What did you say?"

"Your wife is strong to let you go fight fires. I wouldn't be strong enough to let you go."

"You think I'm married?"

"You're wearing a ring, and you said you have to get home to the kids."

"I'm not married anymore. I'm a widower. My wife was killed in a car accident five years ago. I only have my two kids left, Caroline and Jane."

"I'm sorry."

"It's okay. I should really take my ring off. But I feel like if I take it off, she is really gone forever."

"I know what you mean."

"No one could possibly know."

"Something similar happened to my husband."

"Where is your husband?"

I really don't want to get into this conversation. I barely know him. So I'll just play it easy and only say a couple things about it to him.

"He was killed in a car accident about four years ago."

"I'm sorry."

"Don't be."

"Honey, are you ready to go?" Mom asked as she walked in the door. "I'm sorry. I didn't realize you had company."

"It's okay. I was just getting ready to walk out. Mom, this is Keith. He was at the fire. Keith, this is my mom, Casey."

"Hi, it's nice to meet you," Mom said while shaking his hand.

"Nice to meet you too."

Later that evening James called.

"Hey, how did it go with that hot chick?"

"James, is that you?"

"Who else would it be? Wait, were you waiting for a call from that hot chick?"

"That hot chick has a name!" I said with a little bit more force behind my words than I needed to.

"So are you going to answer my question?"

"No, and her name is Alice Carlin."

"Alice Carlin, the ex-supermodel!"

"I don't think so. She has a limp when she walks, and she didn't seem to want a lot of attention on her."

"Alice Carlin was in a car accident."

———

When we arrived home I went straight to my room and looked at pictures of me and Michael. That night I cried myself to sleep. All I could see was the car accident in my dreams. I must have been screaming because Mom came in and woke me up.

"Honey, you're okay."

"I'm sorry, Mom. I didn't mean to wake you."

"Would you like to talk about it?"

"No, that's okay. It's the same dream as always."

"If you ever want to talk, I'll be here."

"What time is it? Do you know?"

"It's almost seven in the morning."

"Thanks. Mom, what did you think of that firefighter?"

"He sounds nice to me; acted like a gentleman."

"Yeah."

"Not the answer you were looking for, was it?"

"No."

"Honey, I cannot answer that question. I do think dating is something you should look at doing again."

"How can you say something like that? I killed my husband and my unborn baby. How can you say that?"

"I can say that because you didn't kill your husband or baby. You made some big decisions in a few seconds. You tried to save your family."

"It has been four years. Why do I still feel so guilty all the time?"

"In order to stop feeling so guilty, you have to forgive yourself. Let Christ back into your heart. Let him heal you."

"You know I don't believe in that stuff anymore."

"You should come to church with me tomorrow."

"If he exists, why didn't he save my husband, or at least my baby, so I could at least have part of my husband with me always?"

"Maybe the baby would have hurt you in the long run. And Michael, remember when I took him to the hospital two months before the accident?"

"Of course; I was so scared I was going to lose him."

"I should have told you this before now. I love you and don't want you to fall apart. I don't want you to get hurt, but I think it's time I told you."

"Tell me what?"

"He fainted because he had low blood sugar, right? Did he tell you they found out that he had cancer when they ran all those tests? The cancer was in his liver."

"He had cancer?"

"They told him he had three years left to live. They said that it was a rare type of cancer and they could try to treat it, but it was unlikely it would work."

"How come you never told me this?"

"Because he made me promise. He said that he would tell you after you had the baby. He didn't want to put more stress on you. As much as I wanted to tell you, I couldn't break that promise to him."

"Michael, why?" I sobbed.

"I'm sorry, honey. I should have told you sooner."

"It's not your fault."

"I know."

"I'm going to see if I can get up on Sarge."

"I'm coming with you."

"Okay. You know, Sarge was Michael's favorite horse. He said that it's because if it hadn't been for him, we would never have met at the fair."

"I'm so sorry. You should try to ride Midnight."

"No! If it weren't for her, I would still have a husband and a baby girl!" I said, crying again.

Midnight was the horse Michael and I were trying to save from her abusive owner. That was the night of the accident. I blame Midnight for the accident, but mostly I blame myself. If I hadn't seen her getting hit and seen that she was a beautiful palomino, my dream horse, we would have never been on that road.

"Be careful."

"I always am. I don't even know if I can get up on Sarge." I tacked Sarge up and got a leg up. It was a little tricky getting my feet in the stirrups, but I got it. When I asked him to gallop, it felt like I was flying as we galloped around the pen.

Chapter 3

"Mom, is this okay to wear to church?"

"You're coming?"

"Is that okay?"

"Yes. What changed your mind?"

"I think it was when I was up on Sarge again. It changed the way I looked at life."

"Let's get going so we can make it on time."

I met James in the parking lot at church. The girls and their aunt were already inside. James and I walked up together to the choir seats.

"Look who's here."

"Where am I supposed to be looking?"

"Up the middle aisle."

It was funny, just seeing her made my stomach do flips. I could not let James see that, so I acted normal.

"Maybe she just moved here."

"Maybe, but now you can get her number."

"James, we are in a church, and I'm not looking for a girlfriend! If you want her number, go get it yourself."

"Okay, I'll get it after church, but only because we have to sing right now."

It was harder to sit through church than I thought it would be. For one thing the hot firefighter, Keith, was there, and the sermon was on feeling guilty. I was almost in tears by the end of the sermon.

As soon as the sermon was done, I said, "Mom, I'll see you at the car."

"Okay. Do you feel all right? You look a little green."

"Yeah."

I walked out of the church before anybody could catch me. I got to the car, and as soon as I was in I let the tears spill out. My left leg was starting to throb because of the long walk to the car.

Somebody knocked on the door. Thinking it was Mom, I unlocked the doors without looking up. All of a sudden my door was open and I was in somebody's arms. *Maybe if I scream somebody will hear me.* I looked up and was surprised to see Keith holding me, with another man right beside him. He must have seen the surprise on my face because he put me down.

"Hello, Keith. You are?"

"Hello, this is James."

"Nice to meet you."

"James, do you really want it?" Keith asked.

"Yes, please," James said.

"Want what?" I asked, confused.

"He wants your phone number," Keith said.

"My phone number?"

"Yes, please," James said quietly.

"No! I'll give Keith my number."

"Keith, get her number and give it to me," James whispered to Keith.

"Sorry, James, but if I give out my number, there are rules that come with it."

"I knew it. You're a model," James said.

"No, I used to be."

"You were in a car accident," James stated.

"Yes. Tell you what. Shut up, and I'll give you my autograph. Sell it on eBay and make a hundred bucks."

"Can I have your picture instead?"

"No, people cannot know I'm here."

I forgot Keith was there until he said, "Why?"

"I ran so the paparazzi wouldn't know where I was. Here comes my mom. I've got to go. Nice to meet you, James. If you wait right here, I'll go and get a photo and a piece of paper from the backseat of the car."

They waited as I got the stuff from the car. I got a picture from the stack in the car and signed it and gave it to James. Then I got out a personal card and gave it to Keith.

"Rule number one: do not give my phone number to anybody. My number is personal. I don't want fans calling me at two in the morning. Rule number two: this applies to both of you. Do not tell anybody where I am, or what I am now, or used to be. Do you understand?" Both of them nodded their heads. "If anybody comes looking for me, I will run, and then the paparazzi will be looking for you to ask you questions and will never leave you alone."

"Why did you give me your number and not James?"

"Because maybe I'm hoping you will call me and let me meet your daughters. I love kids and would love to meet yours. Bye. Mom's in the car."

Chapter 4

As I drove home my phone started to ring. I knew exactly who it was before I even looked at the phone. It was James.

"Hi, James."

"So are you?"

"So am I what?"

"Are you going to call her?"

"Maybe, if I get a girlfriend, will you stop picking on me about women and stay out of my love life? Here's an idea. You go find yourself a girlfriend."

"Yes, but you don't have one, so you're going on a blind date tomorrow night."

"No, it's my night with the kids."

"So? I'm sure if I tell them they can come to my house they would jump at the opportunity."

"Only because you feed them sugar and don't make them go to bed. I'm their dad, and I've got veto power over where they go."

"Don't be mean."

"Cancel the date. I'm calling Alice tonight."

"Do I get to come?"

"If you can find where we will meet at and if she says yes."

"It's a good thing I'm good at following you around in my car."

"Bye, I'm hanging up."

"Okay, see you tomorrow."

About four hours later, I called Alice.

"Hello?" Alice said into the phone.

"Hi, this is Keith."

"Hi, Keith.

"Did you really want to meet my kids?"

"Yes."

"Do you want to meet us at the playground tomorrow at two o'clock?"

"Sure, the one by the school?"

"That's the one."

"Why are you letting me meet your kids?"

"Because you seem like somebody who loves kids … and because I don't want to go on a blind date tomorrow night."

"Okay, see you tomorrow."

All I could think about that night was what Keith's kids would look like. Would they look like him, or would they look like their mother?

"Hey, why are you so dressed up?"

"I'm going to see Rebecca."

"Okay, say hi to her for me."

"I will. Bye."

As I started for the hospital, I calculated how much time

I could be at the hospital. *I'm going to meet Keith and the girls at two this afternoon. If I leave the hospital at a quarter after one, I should get to the park at ten to two.*

When I got to Rebecca's hospital room, I found Rebecca being rude to her nurse.

"Rebecca, what are you doing?"

"She won't take her pills," the nurse replied.

"They make me fall asleep, and I want to talk to you."

"If you don't take your pills, then I'll have to leave. I will call your boyfriend and tell him he can't see you today."

"You wouldn't dare!"

"Want to try me?"

"Fine, give them here!"

"Thank you," the nurse mouthed to me as she walked by to the next person who needed help.

"Rebecca, why do you have to be so difficult?"

"Because I want to go home."

"You can go home tomorrow."

"I want to go home now!"

"Sorry, but one more day. That is if everything goes all right. If you keep refusing to take the pills they give you, they will make you stay."

"Fine, I'll be good."

"Look, Aidan is here. I'll give you some time alone. I'll see you tomorrow." I got out of there sooner than I was planning to, so I took a nice long walk. I was on the left side of the playground when I saw Keith. I walked over and saw who was standing by his sides. There were two brown-haired girls.

"Hi, Keith; these must be your girls."

"Hi, this is Jane and Caroline."

"Hi, girls, I'm Alice."

"Hi, Alice. I'm Jane, and I'm eight years old."

"Hello, Jane, it's nice to meet you, and I'm twenty-nine" Caroline must have thought that was funny because she started to giggle. "May I ask what is so funny?"

"James is right over there making faces at you." She pointed to the parking lot, and when James saw me looking, he pointed somewhere. He was pointing to a bunch of bushes. Then I saw what he was pointing at. It was what I fear most—paparazzi. They found me. I stood up quickly and said, "Keith, you and the girls need to follow me."

"Why?"

"Look at the bushes by the lake." When he glanced over, it hit him; I could see it on his face. "They found me. If you stay here you are going to get hammered with questions you will not be able to answer."

When we started to walk Jane started to throw a fit. "Jane, honey, if you come with us right now, you can have some ice cream when we get to my house." It worked, and she ran to the car. We ran after her.

"Can I get a ride in your car?"

"Yeah, get in. Why do you need a ride? Isn't your car here?"

"My mom dropped me off at the hospital and was going to pick me up there at seven tonight."

"Where am I going?"

"Keep going straight. Girls, do you like horses?" Keith shot me "a what are you doing" look right as the girls yelled, "Yes!"

"That's good because we are going to a horse farm."

"A horse farm?"

"That's where I live. My late husband and I rescued abused horses from their owners."

"Can we ride them? Grandma and Grandpa always used to take us riding," Jane said.

"Sure, as long as it is okay with your dad. Did you ride by yourself or with somebody?"

"Behind Grandma."

"Okay."

⁂

We pulled into Alice's horse farm, and I was shocked. For as far as I could see, it was all horses and pastures. Finally we pulled up to the house. It was not what I was expecting at all. I was expecting a mansion, but it was just a regular farmhouse. As if she could read my mind she said, "Not what you were expecting, is it?"

"No, not really."

"Girls, go into the house and get the ice cream I promised."

"Okay!" Both girls yelled together and jumped out of the car. Alice wasn't far behind them.

⁂

"Just walk in, girls!" I yelled. "I have to go check on something in the barn."

"Can I go with you?" Keith asked.

"I'll give you and the girls a tour after the ice cream. Try to explain what is going on to my mother, please." I ran right to the barn and went into my office. I called 911, and when they answered I told them my name and told them to send officers out to the farm to send off the paparazzi. Then I ran to the house.

When I ran in the door, Mom took me into a big hug and said, "I'm sorry, honey."

"Mom, it was bound to happen sooner or later, so I forewarned the police about a month ago."

"What do you mean forewarned the police? Have you been expecting this?" Keith asked.

"The police know all about me. I've been hiding for almost four years. I feel like I need to tell you about what's going on, so listen carefully. This land was inherited from Michael's family, and when he died he left it to my unborn baby and me. I left this place alone for many years and lived in my other homes with my mom. People started figuring out where I would disappear to when they finally found me again. Nobody knows about this place because it's not something Michael and I bought. They are very good. They will ask around and follow leads to wherever they say. I knew it was only a matter of time. The police are on their way to keep the paparazzi out."

"May I ask what happened to your baby?"

Mom gave him a warning look. I patted her arm, reassuring her it was all right, and whatever was on her mind forgotten. She turned and went back to the kitchen.

"I lost my baby four years ago."

"I'm sorry."

"It's okay. Maybe I'll tell you the whole story someday. If you want any ice cream, then you better get in the kitchen right now."

"The kids won't eat that much ice cream."

"It's not the kids I'm worried about."

"Your mother?"

"Yes, she loves ice cream, and so do I. We fight over it all the time." He laughed at that.

As we walked into the kitchen, I saw my mom emptying the bowl of ice cream into her bowl. "Mom, get out of my ice cream!" I yelled as I ripped the bowl and container out of her hands. Keith and the girls were laughing so hard they had tears running down their cheeks by the time I made it to the other side of the kitchen and across the room from mom. "See what I mean?" I asked Keith.

"Yes, I see, but I'm pretty sure your mom's enjoying that full bowl a lot more than that partial one."

"What! Mom, you suck. I'm not eating anymore. When did you get more ice cream?"

"When I was in town yesterday. When you were up on Sarge."

"Who is Sarge?" asked Jane.

"That is the first horse I ever got."

"Can we see him now?" Caroline asked.

"If it's okay with your dad, I'll give you a tour now. I have to jump up on Sarge later tonight."

"You should ride Midnight too," Mom said before Keith had a chance to respond.

"No!"

"Fine, don't. I'll take Midnight out tonight when you take out Sarge."

"As long as you stay away from me and Sarge."

"Can we have our tour now?" Caroline asked.

"Yes, of course."

I took the girls to the arena and told them to stand up on the loading platform. I told Keith to close the north side barn doors and flip the switch to the left of the doors. Keith did as I said and then went to where his daughters were. I went and opened the south side doors.

Chapter 5

The girls and I were standing on some sort of platform, and Alice was standing in the middle of the arena. She started to whistle a tune. It took me a while to realize what she was whistling, but I finally figured out she was whistling "God's Been Good to Me." All of a sudden it sounded like a herd of elephants was coming, but it was a herd of horses. I could hear Alice calling out Sarge's name. All of a sudden this black horse stepped up to her, and she backed up and jumped on that huge stallion.

"You okay, Keith? You look a little white."

"How many are in here?"

"About twenty. I should have probably warned you of what I was planning on doing."

"Yeah, maybe."

"Let me saddle him up."

"Okay, see you in five minutes."

"How about two minutes?"

"What? Nobody can saddle a horse that size that fast."

"Are you challenging me?"

"Yes."

"I wouldn't do that if I were you," Casey said as she walked in the arena.

"Mom, don't interfere. If Keith wants to challenge me, let him."

"Are you going to challenge her?"

"Yes, I don't believe you."

"If I can, you have to get on a horse and ride with your daughters."

"If you don't?"

"You get to pick out a horse for me to try to get up on and try to get it to do barrels or jumps."

"Deal."

"Boy, you're in for a show," Casey said quietly.

"I'll get the stopwatch and tack."

"I'll come with you."

"No, stay with the girls. Sarge, stand."

She started to whistle again, and all the horses except Sarge left. When she came back, she had her tack and stopwatch with her. She told me to start the stopwatch when she had all her stuff laid out. It was amazing. Her horse did exactly the right stuff at the right time. All of a sudden she yelled, "Stop!" I looked down. One minute and forty-five seconds.

"Holy cow!"

"I'll go get Ghost, Angel, and Twilight."

"Okay, how did you learn to saddle like that?"

"Keith, you're looking at the all-girl rodeo queen before she went into modeling. When Sarge and I went, we had to be able to tack up, jump on, and run the barrels."

"Now you tell me that story."

"Well, I had to get you on a horse somehow."

***

Just when I was ready to leave, Mom came in riding on Midnight. I don't know what emotion hit me first, if it was anger, hurt, or most of all fear.

"Mom, get her out. Sarge!" I screamed. Sarge looked up on alert and then ran at a mad dash for me. I yelled, "Rescue!" Sarge ran past me full speed, and I hopped on him and we ran out of the arena.

***

I walked up to Casey. When I looked at her face, I thought I could see worry and sorrow.

"What just happened with this horse and Alice?"

"That's a story you'll have to get from Alice. Telling you would make me break a promise to my daughter."

"Why did she scream when she saw the horse? She told you that you could ride her."

"She told me not to bring Midnight by Sarge."

"Sarge didn't seem to mind Midnight being in here with him."

"Sarge knows that Midnight would not hurt him. It's Alice who does not like Midnight, and she would be with Sarge, so she used him as an excuse. This is not my story to tell you, Keith. When she is ready, she will tell you."

"Okay, I'll get the story from her one day."

As I walked in with Angel, Ghost, Twilight, and Sarge, I heard the end of Mom and Keith's conversation. When I was sure Mom had left, I walked back into the barn.

When I walked in with the horses, the girls jumped up and down and spooked the horses. The horses reared up and down.

"Girls, stop jumping; settle down. Sarge, at ease! Twilight, Angel, down, girls. Ghost, you're fine. It's going to be okay. Nobody is going to hurt you," I said in the most soothing voice I could.

"Are you sure they are safe to ride?"

"Yes, the girls just frightened them. You have to remember where these horses come from. They have been abused by their owners, so they can get scared by a lot of movements."

"Okay, I see now; they were having flash backs of being abused with all the noise, so they were trying to get away so they wouldn't be hit."

"Exactly; now, girls, walk up very slowly to me." The girls did exactly as I said. "Jane, you're going to ride Angel; and, Caroline, you're going to ride Twilight."

"Okay, I get Sarge, right? Please, don't make me ride that huge horse," Keith said.

"Chicken! Girls, just let them sniff you. Nobody rides Sarge except me."

"That was a mean trick you played."

"Would I have gotten you on a horse any other way?"

"No."

"I just set up a proper saddle system, and you did the rest."

"That is mean. How am I getting up on that huge thing?"

"I'll show you. Sarge, stand still." I took a running start and jumped and landed square on Sarge's back. "Sarge, walk on." I walked up to Ghost and grabbed his halter and walked him up to the landing. "Just swing your leg over him and tell him to stand."

"I can do that. I don't think I could have done what you just did."

I started to laugh. "You don't think I'm that mean, do you? It took me ten years to get that down, and Sarge is the only horse I can do that to."

"It's good to hear you laugh again," Mom said as she walked into the barn.

"Mom, will you get my hat?" As she walked away I got the girls up on their horses. "Thanks, I'm going to go barrel. Mom will give you lessons. That is her favorite thing to do."

⁓

We got our lessons from Casey, and she told us to go watch Alice barrel. We all gasped when we saw her. She took off at a dead run, and when she neared the barrels it sounded like she said, "Ha!"

"What do you say when you near the barrels?" I asked her when she came over to me.

"Do you want me to say the word?"

"Yes."

"Ha!" she said, and Sarge spun and sent rocks flying at me. They came back at a trot.

"Thanks for the rock shower."

"Hey, don't get mad at me. You asked me to say it. I already told you that Sarge acts on commands, not pressure.

I have to take him through the jumps. You can watch if you want or go up to the house."

"I'll watch."

"Okay, suit yourself. We will jump for half an hour, and then we all can load up and go for a ride."

We were coming up to the five-foot jump when I saw them. The paparazzi got past the police. As we sailed over the jump they got some good shots. Sarge wasn't sure what to do. He knew not to go out of pattern. When I yelled, "Follow lead!" he went off path and let me direct him to the gates. As we neared the gate, I yelled at Keith, "Open the gates!" Right when we got there he got the gate undone, but we ignored it. We just jumped over the fence and were running to the barn's protection.

"What is going on?" Keith yelled as I ran past him.

When I got down and Keith made it into the barn I said, "The paparazzi got past the police. I saw them get some good pictures. It's going to be hell tomorrow. I'll warn you now. Stay inside, or hang out with me tomorrow. I will be surrounded by personal bodyguards."

"I'll ask the girls."

"If you come with me we can go wherever you want; you just have to be by my side constantly. They won't bother the girls because they could get in some serious trouble by the police."

"We'll ask the girls." We took off at a dead run up to the house and found the girls and Mom eating my cookies.

"Mom, I need to talk with you."

"Okay, be right there." She walked cautiously up to where I was at in the living room.

"The paparazzi are getting by the police. They got some good pictures of Sarge and me jumping over the five-foot jump. It might be safer for you to go to Texas and stay at the mansion. It's going to be a zoo here tomorrow. I have to stay and protect the people I have involved in this. It will give me a taste of old times."

"I'll get the plane ready if that's what you want me to do.

"Yes, please."

I went to change. I went to my closet and pulled out stuff I haven't worn in a long time. One was a full-length baby blue dress. It was the one I was wearing when I met Michael. The one I decided on wearing was a full-length red halter top dress, and I put on the matching jewelry. When I was done with that, I went to the bathroom and put on my makeup.

When I was done I walked into the kitchen and had the pleasure of watching Keith's eyes pop out of his head. "Okay, what do you want to do?"

"Why did you get so dressed up?"

"If the paparazzi are taking pictures, then I have to look nice. If I ever want to get back into modeling, the people that are going to hire me will look back at the magazines."

"Girls, what do you want to do tomorrow?"

"Can we come to Alice's house tomorrow?"

"Sounds good to me if it's okay with Alice.

"It's fine with me. I'm making my mom go to Texas."

"What's in Texas?" Keith asked.

"My mansion and personal bodyguards for both Mom

and me. She'll send my guards and half of the house guards back to me and will keep hers."

"Okay, see you tomorrow. What time do you want to meet us and where?"

"I have to get Rebecca out of the hospital tomorrow morning. If I'm not there to get her, she will probably kill me. If she doesn't, her nurse probably will. Do you want to meet me at the hospital at around nine tomorrow morning?"

"That sounds good." And with that they left. I helped Mom pack her bag to get her to Texas.

"Do you want me to send back all the house guards?"

"No, just send half of them. I don't need all two hundred of them. Make sure you send Jenna, Mandy the cook, and Tyler."

"Why do you want Mandy?"

"I want Mandy because I'm sending the best cook to Texas, and I don't want to eat junk food the whole time that you are gone. I can't cook, remember?"

Chapter 6

When I got home I called James. When he didn't answer, I left a voice message. "Hey, James, it's Keith. Call me back as soon as you get this." Right after I hung up, the house phone rang.

"Daddy, there's a guy on the phone for you," Jane said.

"Did you get the person's name?"

"No."

"Okay, thank you." When I answered the phone, I was bombarded with a bunch of questions at the same time. I hung up the phone and told the girls to not answer the phone. I called Alice; she answered on the second ring. "Why am I getting phone calls and getting questions thrown at me before I can answer the first one?"

"Keith, you can't answer any of those questions. They are paparazzi and my fans. You can't give them any information about me. People that need to get ahold of you know your cell phone number right?"

"Of course."

"Good, then unplug your house phone and lock all your doors and windows. I'm doing the same thing here."

"How did they figure out where I live?"

"They tracked your photo, I'm guessing."

"But how did they get my number? My number is not in the phonebook."

"They have their ways. Talk to you tomorrow."

"Okay." When I hung up, I did as she directed me to do. Then I called James and told him to do the same thing. "Girls, what do you want to do?"

"Play Horseopoly!" Caroline yelled.

"Yeah," Jane echoed.

"Okay."

After a few heated games of Horseopoly, I sent the kids to bed. It didn't take long and I was in bed sleeping and dreaming about Alice jumping on Sarge and how she looked.

As we started out to the north pasture, we saw the plane fly overhead, so we made the horses go into a dead run to the plane.

"Call me when you land."

"Okay, I'll send back the guards."

"Don't forget to find out what shots they got and are in the papers. Send them to me when you find out, will you?"

"I won't forget. Got to go."

As she loaded on to the plane, a million lights flashed from the bushes. I grabbed Twilight and made her and Sarge run together on the way back to the house.

When I got the horses untacked and in their pastures for the night, I went to the house. I got ready for bed and made sure I locked all the doors. When I was positive every thing was locked up, I went to bed. I caught myself dreaming about Keith and the girls.

I was about to have Keith run the barrels on Ghost when there was this ringing. I woke up from my dream almost immediately. Then I remembered. Mom was to call when she landed. I grabbed my cell phone and answered it. "Hello?"

"Hi, I landed safely. You sound like I woke you up."

"You did. I'm glad you called. Did you send the guards?"

"Yes. They should be there by ten tomorrow morning, just in time to go to the rodeo."

"Rodeo!" *Tomorrow morning is the rodeo. This will be the last time I ride for Michael. I have to move on with my life.* "Mom, tomorrow is the open show, right?"

"Yes, tomorrow is the open-show rodeo."

"No! What bad timing."

"Why is it bad timing?"

"Tomorrow, Keith and the girls are coming over at nine o'clock. We're meeting at the hospital because I have to get Rebecca."

"So take Keith and the girls to the rodeo with you and Rebecca. Have one of your guards take the horses up there for you. Make sure you have horses for everybody to ride in the rodeo."

"Mom, you are a lifesaver."

"No, I'm not. I have just been in a situation like that, but it was with your father and my best friend."

"Thanks, I'd love to talk longer, but I have an early morning tomorrow."

"Night, honey; sleep well."

"You too, Mom." And with that we hung up and I went back to bed. When I finally fell asleep, I picked up where my dream left off.

Chapter 7

When I woke the next morning I quickly got dressed. Somebody was knocking on the door. I went to answer it, and when I opened the doors I was surprised to see my guards. Since I had my guards, I told the police to go home, and I finished getting ready. When I was done I took off for the hospital.

"Hi, Rebecca. Are you ready to go home?"

"Yes, can we go to your house?"

"Yes, if you don't mind my bodyguards and the paparazzi."

"Paparazzi and bodyguards?"

"They found me again."

"Okay, can we go home? I'm sick of this place."

"Do you mind going to the rodeo with Keith, the girls, and I, or would you rather I dropped you off at home first?"

"Back up. Who is Keith?"

"Keith is the really hot firefighter that saved your life and who has two adorable girls."

"Is he married?"

"No, his wife was killed in a car accident."

"Okay, I'll go with. I want to meet him."

"Well, we have to get out of here first."

"That's easy. You just walk out."

"You have paperwork to sign, and since I'm not your husband, I can't do it for you."

"I don't have a husband, so hand me the paperwork." She signed all the papers, and we got out of there. As soon as we set foot outside the hospital, my guards surrounded us immediately. The cameras started, and all they got was my guards.

Some of them started yelling, "Let us get an interview and pictures."

"What time is it?" I asked my guards.

"Nine o'clock," one of them answered.

"Keith should be here any minute," I told Rebecca. When I said that I looked at the entrance and saw Keith's vehicle pulling in the parking lot. "That's Keith right there," I said, pointing at the entrance.

"Let's go meet him."

"Hi, Keith and girls."

"Hi, Alice and Rebecca."

"He knows me?" Rebecca asked.

"He did save you from the fire, remember?"

"Hi, Alice," Caroline spoke up, giggling.

"Hi, Caroline. This is Rebecca. Is James making funny faces at me again?"

"No, but he is right there." I turned around to see James trying to get past my security guards. I had to laugh when they threw him on the ground.

"Hi, Jane. Come here. I have a secret," I whispered in her ear. "If we can convince your daddy to let us go to the rodeo today, I've got horses there waiting to be ridden. Would you like to go?" She nodded eagerly. "Should we let your sister in on the secret and see what she thinks?" She nodded again. "How about you go tell her, and I'll distract your daddy. Make sure you make up a plan." Jane went and told Caroline the plan. She nodded eagerly too.

"Do I get to hear the secret too?" Keith asked me. The girls and I shook our heads at the same time. His facial expression was hurt. I had to laugh.

"You are the one the secret is about."

"That's okay. I'll get it out of the girls later."

"No you won't."

"Do I get to hear the secret?" Rebecca asked me.

"You already know the secret."

"What secret?" James asked from right outside my circle of guards. "Can I come in?"

"Let him in," I told the guards. The guards opened a space big enough to let in James.

"If you tell James, then you have to tell me," Keith said. His voice sounded a little hurt and hopeful.

"Not a problem, because we're not telling James. Are we, girls?"

"Right!" the girls and Rebecca said at the same time.

"Girls, what's the plan?" The girls ran over to me and started to whisper in my ear. "Hold on one second, girls. Rebecca, would you distract Keith and James?"

"Sure, what do you want me to do with them?"

"Just talk to them." I walked over to the girls, and they started whispering again.

"I think that you go and give daddy a kiss and tell him he is coming," Caroline said. I started laughing.

"I think we just walk up to him, tell him we're taking him somewhere, and you drive us there," Jane said. I started to laugh again.

"You know what I'm thinking?"

"What?" Jane asked.

"Do you know his cell phone number?"

"Yes," Caroline said.

"Will you type it in my phone?"

"Yes." Caroline took my cell phone and put in his number. I ran to Rebecca.

"Can I use your cell phone?"

"Sure." She handed me her phone and gave me a questioning look. I ran back to the girls.

In the phone I texted, "Will you go to the rodeo with me?" and put in Keith's number. I sent it and watched for Keith's expression.

———

The girls and Alice were being very secretive. My phone started ringing, and when I opened it up it read, "Will you go to the rodeo with me?" I must have had a weird expression on my face because all of the girls started laughing. James had the same confused expression that must have been on my face.

"Let me see the phone," Rebecca said. In the phone she typed, "I would love to," and sent it.

"What did you do that for? I don't even know that number."

"I'm pretty sure you know the person."

"No, I don't know that number."

"I hope you don't know that number, because it's mine."

"Why would someone use your phone to text me?"

"Because you would know her phone number. The person who sent that text is the one responsible for all the guards." Then everything started falling into place—the girls being so secretive. Alice wanting Rebecca's phone.

"Rebecca, why did you have to ruin it? Girls, now." The girls ran over to me and started to beg.

"Okay, we can go to the rodeo."

"We need to go so I can tack up the horses."

"So you can tack up the horses?"

"You didn't think that we were going to just watch it, did you? It's open-show rodeo, and I'm registered. Hopefully you will let me sign you and the girls up for some activities."

Chapter 8

"Have you seen her tack a horse?" Rebecca asked Keith.

"How do you think she got me on a horse?"

"He didn't believe me and walked into his own trap by challenging me." Rebecca started to laugh. "When I did it, I told him the story."

"That is so mean, but so funny."

"It was very mean, and then she put me on Ghost."

"What's wrong with Ghost?"

"You just opened up a can of something you probably didn't want to," I said.

"Why?"

"Ghost is Rebecca's favorite horse."

"I've seen how she is with the nurses, and I think I better run."

"Good idea. Run for the rodeo."

"By the way, good joke."

"Whatever; Rebecca, girls, James, let's go to the rodeo." We started toward the rodeo, and I realized that I had five minutes. I told everybody to hurry. When we came to the gates, I told them my name. They took a look at everybody and then let us in. I ran to my trailer and got into my riding uniform and then ran and unloaded the horses. Once I got Ghost out, Rebecca came and got him and started tacking her own horse. I got the rest of them unloaded and tied to the trailer and tacked them up too. I put the girls up on their horses, and I got up on Sarge. Rebecca hopped up on Ghost. "James, you can get up on Leo if you want. If you don't want to and you see Keith, tell him I expect to see him on Leo."

"Okay, I'll tell Keith. How did you get him on a horse?"

"Let's just say Keith isn't very good at making bets."

"You're telling me."

"You asked. I've got to go. I'm going to be up."

"Knock their socks off. Keith said that you were really good."

"Thanks." With that, I rode up to the arena. They called my name as soon I came to a stop. I walked into the arena, and the announcer said, "The old all-girl rodeo champion." With that, Sarge and I took off to the first barrel.

We rounded the first barrel and made it perfectly. Sarge did exactly what he was supposed to do. He went where I was looking. We rounded the second barrel and dashed for the third barrel. We rounded it, and we were on the home stretch. The audience was quiet. I could feel Sarge's heart pumping almost as clearly as I could feel mine. I could feel the adrenaline pumping through my veins. I urged Sarge as fast as he could go. *This is going to be the last run I do for Michael and my baby. I have to find someone else to love and to do my runs for. I have to make myself public again in order to get on with my life so I can find that somebody.*

As we crossed the line the buzzer went off. Sarge whipped into a circle, and we waited for the score. The crowd was still really quiet, waiting for the outcome. We got fourteen seconds. The crowd went wild and so did the cameras. I made Sarge trot out of the pen.

As soon as we were out, my bodyguard surrounded me and Sarge. I hopped down and noticed Keith staring at the scoreboard, which still had my score on it.

"I didn't realize you were that good."

"Well, you did see me run. I just didn't let Sarge go all he could. We are still a little rusty. Rebecca, will you cool off Sarge?"

"Sure; what do I say to the paparazzi?"

"Just tell them I hired you, and continue cooling off Sarge. Say that if you don't continue, you will be fired."

"Okay, here; take Ghost."

"Come on, girls. Keith, let's go get something to drink." The girls were right behind me. Somewhere along the line they were pulled off their horses.

When we got back to the trailer, everybody hopped inside, except for my guards. When Rebecca was done cooling off Sarge, she came in. We sat in there in complete silence until there was a knock on the door. I cracked the door, and Tyler, my bodyguard, said, "He says his name is James."

"What does he look like?"

"Blond, shorter than the guy in there by a little bit." I glanced at Keith. He nodded his head.

"Let him in." When James entered he was swearing.

"James, there are kids in hearing range, and I'm in hearing range. You say it again, and I will have to wash your mouth out with soap. And if you give me trouble I'm sure my guards will help me."

"I'd like to see you try."

"Are you challenging me?" Keith was about to say something when I cut him off with a wave of my hand.

"I said I'd like to see you try, not that I wanted you to do it."

"Is that a yes or a no?"

"That is a yes."

"Keith, will you move the girls outside to the cookies?"

"Yes, ma'am."

"I'll help," Rebecca volunteered. When they up and left, I approached James.

"Let's make this a little bit more interesting."

"Okay, just to be clear, you're not going to use your guards, right?"

"That is correct."

"Okay, let's bet."

"If I win, you have to ride a horse."

"If you don't?"

"What will it be?"

"I get your phone number."

"Deal!"

"Deal!" We shook hands. I took one fist into his gut and made him drop to his knees on the floor. I spun around and karate chopped his back. He dropped down on all fours. I grabbed his head between my left arm and grabbed the bar of soap off the counter by the sink with the other and shoved it in his mouth.

Alice kicked us out of the trailer. "Who do you think will win the bet?" I asked Rebecca.

"I think Alice will win."

"I don't know. James is a pretty good fighter."

"Does he have a black belt in karate?"

"No, does she?"

"Yes, when she went into modeling she took karate classes. It got to the point her instructor wouldn't fight with her because she always won."

"Okay, I think she will win, knowing that piece of information. What do you think the bet will be?"

"Knowing Alice, she will make him ride a horse … which will explain why her small horse trailer is coming over here. What do you think his side of the bet will be?"

"I think it will be her phone number. When he asked for it, she wouldn't give it to him. She said she would only give her phone number to me. When I got the phone number, I also got the rules."

"What? She gave you her phone number but not James?" she asked, and when I nodded my head, she started laughing hysterically.

James was obviously expecting to win, because when I let him up he just sat there with the soap still in his mouth. I spun and grabbed my camera and snapped a picture.

When I got it saved, I ran out of the trailer, laughing my head off.

"What are you laughing so hard at?" Keith asked. When I couldn't answer him I gave him the camera. Keith started laughing too. Rebecca grabbed the camera from Keith and took one look at it and started to giggle. James came walking slowly out of the trailer, and we started to laugh harder.

"Where did you learn to fight like that?" James asked me. Rebecca was the one to answer him.

"Say hello to Ms. Black Belt, whose teacher wouldn't fight her anymore because she always beat him."

"You could have told me that story before I fell into the trap."

"Hey, you started the trap and you fell into your own trap. You didn't ask about my history, and I simply didn't open up and tell you. "

"James, don't argue with her. She bet you fair and square, and if you try she will win. Remember, I fell into the same trap," Keith said.

"You both fell into your own traps. What do you have to do?"

"He has to ride Dakota." When I said that, I looked over at the small trailer. Midnight was being unloaded. I screamed and ran back to my big trailer.

When Alice looked over at the trailer and screamed, I new exactly what had happened. They had brought Midnight.

I saw Rebecca turn around and tell them to reload Midnight. After she told them, she ran to Alice's trailer.

I looked up and saw about twenty guards surrounding somebody. What had Alice said the other night? "I'm sending Mom to Texas, and she will send back my guards and keep hers." It was Casey. I walked over to her.

"Hi, Casey."

"Hi, Keith. Why are they loading Midnight back up?"

"Rebecca told them to when Alice saw Midnight and screamed. She ran to the trailer and locked the door."

"No."

"Did you bring Dakota?"

"Yes. I got home right when the call came in. So I loaded up Dakota and Midnight and came. I called and reserved Midnight some spots about a month ago. I was hoping I could get Alice on her, but I think we know that answer." Rebecca came walking over.

"Hi, Casey. Keith, will you see if you can get her to unlock the door?" Rebecca asked, her voice sounding a little hopeful.

"If you can't get her to open up, what makes you think she would open up for me?"

"She will listen to a guy. She respects you," Casey said.

"I can only try." I walked to the trailer and knocked on the door. "Alice, will you open the door? Your mom's really worried."

"Why did she bring her here?"

"I think that is a question for your mom to answer. Will you open up?" I heard the lock being undone. I waved Casey and Rebecca over. When she swung the door open we all jumped in at once. When everybody was in and the door was shut I called James on my cell phone. He answered on the first ring. "Will you entertain the girls for a while?" I asked.

"Tell him to get the ice cream out of my truck for the girls," Casey said.

"Hey, Casey said that you were supposed to get the ice cream out of the truck for the girls."

"Okay, I'll entertain the girls for a while."

"Thank you." I hung up.

I opened the door for Keith, and all three came in. Keith was the first to speak, "Casey, maybe you should tell Alice why you brought Midnight."

"Alice, are you going to tell him the story yet?"

"No!"

"I brought her here because she is signed up in the rodeo."

"I didn't sign her up."

"No, you didn't. I did."

"Why?"

"I was hoping you would ride her."

"Mom, that horse is a killer. I will not ride that horse."

"No, she's not a killer and neither are..." She trailed off, but I didn't need her to finish what she was saying. She was going to say, "And neither are you."

"Mom, don't go there please." I forgot Keith and Rebecca were there until Rebecca spoke up.

"Don't go where? If we are talking about the accident, I would like to add to it. I know you didn't kill your husband or unborn baby, no matter what you believe," Rebecca said. I saw Keith's eyes flash with an emotion, but he quickly hid it. I knew I had to escape.

"I'm pretty sure that if I don't get James and Keith on horses now, I never will."

"I'll get on a horse, and so will James. If I'm on a horse and call him chicken a few times, he will realize his bad-boy image is going down the drain."

"That will work until you see the horse you're riding."

"What? I'm not riding Ghost?"

"Ghost is mine!" Rebecca said harshly.

"No, you'll be riding Leo."

"Who's Leo?"

"Leo is a very gentle horse. Keith, I'd like to enter the girls in egg and spoon."

"What's egg and spoon?"

"The girls would be up on their horses and have a spoon with an egg on it and they have to ride around the arena. If the egg falls off the spoon, then they are out. You want to be the last one with the egg on your spoon."

"Sounds like fun."

"It is. I'd like to enter you, Rebecca, Mom, and me in four in a line."

"Sounds challenging."

"I'm in!" Rebecca said, sounding very excited.

"I'm in," Mom said.

"Keith, if you don't want to do it, I'm sure I can find some hot cowboy to do it with us."

"I'll do it."

I couldn't help but say I'd do it. The thought of her working with some cowboy made my stomach turn to acid.

I called James and told him to bring the girls back. As we waited for them, Alice tacked up all the horses except Ghost and Midnight. Casey took Midnight on the side of the trailer that Alice couldn't see and tacked her up. Rebecca tacked Ghost, who was standing by Twilight. All I could do was stand and stare at Leo. He was huge.

"James, you ready to get on a horse? You lost the bet. Keith, Leo is ready for you," I heard Alice call.

"Okay, I'll jump up on him in a second. Let me get the girls on their horses."

"Keith, are you stalling? The girls are already up."

"Yes. James, get up on Dakota! You lost that bet fair and square."

"Shut up, Keith!"

"James, do I have to wash your mouth out with soap again?" Alice asked.

"I bet you didn't get that picture with the soap in my mouth. I bet you missed."

"How much you wanna bet?" That was it. I started laughing.

"What's all this talk about mouths being washed out with soap?" Casey asked.

"Before you came, James came in that trailer swearing because of Alice's bodyguards."

Casey interrupted me. "I bet that went over well. Alice doesn't like swearing. I get in trouble all the time for it."

"She didn't. She asked him if he needed her to wash his mouth out with soap. James walked right into his own trap."

"Please tell me he didn't bet against my daughter. "

"He did. Alice made everybody get out of the trailer except James. When Alice got the soap in his mouth, he sat there in shock, and she got a picture of him sitting there with the soap in his mouth. They made a few bets. Alice said James had to ride a horse. And James said … what did you say she had to do?"

"She was supposed to give me her number." Both Casey and I started laughing. "What?"

"Look behind you," I said. Alice was standing in the doorway with a huge picture in her hands. It was the picture of him kneeling at her feet with a bar of soap in his mouth. "When did you get that done?" I yelled to her.

"I have a printer in the trailer."

"Fine, put it away. You got the picture. I'll ride the horse," James said. She tossed the picture back into the trailer and jogged over to him.

"James, you know how you wanted a picture of me."

"Since I was a good sport, do I get one now?"

"Sure, you can have that one with you kneeling at my feet with a bar of soap in your mouth." Everybody started to laugh except for James and the girls. The girls didn't laugh because they didn't know what was going on.

"I don't want that picture."

"James, are you pouting? Let's get you both up on horses. Rebecca got the girls up and they are practicing again. Keith, you need to get up on Leo and start to learn the pattern. It's set up over there." She pointed to the left. "When I get James going, I'll come over and help you. When you've got it down we'll call over Mom and Rebecca." She walked over to Dakota and brought him up for James.

"He's huge!"

"No, he's just a normal-sized horse. Be careful what you say. You might hurt his feelings. I don't know if he would kick you or not. He never liked Michael."

"That sure boosts my confidence."

"To get on you have to put your leg right here and just swing your other leg over and put it in here."

"Why did I make this bet?" James grumbled to himself.

"If you kick his sides gently, he will go. If you lay your reins on his neck he will turn that direction." By the time she mounted Sarge, the paparazzi were coming to talk to James. So she let him escape to the safety of the trailer.

"Are you ready to learn the pattern and stop shaking your head at James? It isn't his fault the paparazzi are scary people."

I didn't realize I was shaking my head.

"Leo knows the pattern, but you need to learn it too. Ready to play follow the leader? I'll start with a walk, but you're going to have to get comfortable with doing this at a run."

"Okay, let's do this."

He looked a little scared when I told him to pick up the pace. He worked up the courage, though, and went through it all in a trot. It looked like he was getting it. I called over Rebecca and Mom.

Mom came over riding on Midnight. She walked very slowly. She was carrying something that she gave to a nearby guard.

Rebecca came running over to me on Ghost. "Where do you want me?"

"I was trying to decide what order I should put everybody in. I'm going to run Sarge through and see how he does." I ran Sarge through. We tripped a little in the beginning. I stopped and checked his hooves. In his right hoof there was a rock. I led him back to the trailer. When I got the rock picked out, I saw he had a cut on his left hind leg. It didn't look too bad, but when I went to touch his leg he shied away; and when he finally let me touch it, it felt warm. "Rebecca, I'm not going to be able to ride Sarge anymore."

"Why?" Rebecca asked as she came riding up.

"Sarge has a cut on his left hind leg, and it feels warm around it."

"That sucks. Will we have to pull out of four in a line?"

"Maybe. I'll have to pull out of jumping. Sarge is the only one who can jump."

"No, Midnight can jump. Take her for jumping and quickly train Dakota for four in a line. I'll take Midnight up to lead and then have Leo, Ghost, and let Dakota take up the back. He knows how to play 'follow the leader,' and the other horses know the pattern," Mom said. I hadn't realized she had come over.

"I can train Dakota in, but I will not ride Midnight."

"You have to get over your grudge against Midnight."

"No!"

"Fine, don't ride her. I did bring back the things you wanted me to mail to you."

"The magazines?"

"Yeah, they got some good pictures of Keith, you, and the girls at the park."

"How about Sarge jumping?"

"They got a few." I motioned for the magazines. When I was paging through the magazine, I saw a picture of the car accident. I stopped and read. The article said:

Alice Carlin was found in a little town called Evansville Minnesota. When Alice recovered from her accident, she left hurting. Her husband and unborn baby were killed in the car accident. Michael Carlin, the husband, was alive when the ambulance got there, but Alice was unconscious.

Michael's side of the car was completely smashed in. Michael had thrown himself over his wife and unborn baby, trying to protect them. He was willing to die for them. When they got Michael out, he kept repeating the words, "It's not your fault, honey." When they got him in the ambulance, his dying words were, "Don't blame yourself, honey. It's not your fault. Take care of our baby. I will always love you."

On the way to the hospital, Alice came around. She kept saying, "Save my baby. My stomach hurts so bad. Michael, where are you?" The doctors told her that she had to move her hands so they could look at the baby. When she finally let them, they said the baby was dead. She was eight months pregnant. The doctors were getting ready to do a C-section at the hospital, but they were too late.

The doctors are saying Michael killed the baby by throwing himself over the baby and his wife.

I hadn't realized how hard I was sobbing until Mom pried the magazine from my hands and handed it to Rebecca. Then she grabbed me in a hug and led me to the trailer.

When we entered the trailer, I fell to the floor, sobbing, saying, "Michael didn't kill my baby. He was trying to protect us." Mom came over and pulled me off the floor and let me sob on her.

"Rebecca, will you go load up the horses? We're going home," Mom said.

"Yes, I'm so sorry, Alice," Rebecca said as she walked out of the trailer.

"Honey, they don't know what they are talking about. They're just trying to sell magazines. Right now you are the hot topic."

"Why did they have to say that about Michael? He would never have hurt me or the baby. He wasn't going to let me drive, but I insisted because he wasn't feeling well."

"I'm sorry, honey. Nobody should have to go through what you are going through right now."

"I don't want to go home yet. I want to go through with the stuff I have signed up to do."

"Okay, let's go kick some cowboys' butts. Let's go unload the horses again."

I went to the trailer to check on Alice. "Hey, what happened? You said you had to go back to the trailer and would be right back. Then Rebecca came out and started to load all the horses and said we're going home."

"Sarge has a cut on his left hind leg and can't run. We aren't going home. I was looking at a magazine and got a little shaken up about what they wrote in there about me."

"The girls will be up soon."

"I need to try to train in Dakota for four in a line. I want to get that done before the girls are up for egg and spoon."

"How long do you think it will be before four in a line?"

"I don't know. It's egg and spoon, then key, the ribbon race, and finally four in a line." With that, she turned and walked away and got up on Dakota.

I was trying to get Dakota to do the pattern, but he was shying away from the barrels. When I glanced back toward the trailers, Keith was the only one there. It was a good thing I taught Keith the pattern before. "Keith, grab a horse and come here."

"What horse should I grab?"

"Either Leo or Ghost." Keith turned and grabbed Leo. He hopped on and came riding over. "I need you to walk the pattern in front of Dakota. He's scared of the barrels. He needs to be shown that they are not going to eat him."

"Okay, you ready?"

"Let's go. We have approximately five minutes to get this done."

"Why only five?"

"The girls will be up, and I want to watch them ride."

"Let's go."

We followed Leo perfectly. We were halfway on the sixth round through when they called egg and spoon.

"Come on, break the pattern. Let's go watch the girls," I said. Keith and I bolted for the competition arena at the same time. We got there and found out the girls were next. It was the senior competition, then the juniors, then the girls.

When I glanced over, I saw the girls on their horses and James on foot. Then it hit me. I hadn't gotten James on a horse yet. "Keith, we have about fifteen minutes until the girls are up. Let's get James on a horse."

"Let's do it! I have a lot of paybacks to give him."

"Don't be mean."

"I won't be *too* mean."

We rode over to James. I hopped off Dakota and told James to get up. Keith didn't do very well at hiding his laugh when James asked me, "How?"

"Shut up, Keith. You asked me pretty much the same question when I brought Ghost in for you to ride." It was James's turn to laugh at Keith. "You put your foot in here." I pointed to the stirrups. He did as I directed. "Then you push up and swing your leg over the horse. You put your foot in the stirrup right here." James was up in the saddle, and I took the lead rope from Twilight and hooked it on to Dakota and gave it to Keith.

"No, you can't give that to Keith. He will make me get bucked off."

"Keith, will you hop off of Leo? I'll give James his first ride." Keith hopped off Leo, and I hopped on. "Are you ready?"

"Yes." With that, I took off in a dead run to the other side of the pasture. James started screaming behind me, so I swung around and told him to stop screaming. "Are you sure you want me to lead you around? I don't like to go slow."

"No, I want Keith back."

"Good." I flagged Keith over. "He changed his mind. Are you still willing to give him a lesson?"

"Sure. James, you are a chicken that screams like a little girl." I started to laugh and walked away.

James was doing pretty well with his lessons, so I stopped and unhooked the lead rope.

"Um, Keith, what are you doing?"

"I'm giving you free rein to go wherever you want."

"Is that a good idea?"

"Yeah, you're doing fine." With that, I walked away. I went back to the arena and was surprised to see that Alice was not there. I didn't have time to go look for her because the girls were just called up to do egg and spoon. Casey sent me to go get James.

When I got to James, I told him, "The girls are up next if you want to see them."

"Okay, race you up there."

"You're on. Let's go."

I was walking up to the trailer from giving James the first worst ride of his life when I neared the trailer. A horse whinnied at me. I look up and almost fell over. I was surprised to see it was Midnight. Why was she whinnying at me?

Was Michael trying to send me a message? I walked over to her, and she put her head into my hand. I started to scratch her head. When I glanced at the trailer, a magazine was sitting there.

It was the one I had been reading before when Mom had ripped it out of my hands because I was crying so hard. I opened it up and found the article again. I started to read where I left off.

If Michael did kill the baby, it wasn't intentional.

We interviewed a couple people about what they think, and here are some of their answers. "I think it is the mother's fault the baby is dead. Being eight months pregnant is not a time to be driving a car."

When Alice's mother got to the hospital, she wouldn't answer any of our questions. She ran to her daughter's side and had her bodyguards stand outside the hospital door. The only people let in were her mother, best friend, Rebecca, the doctors, and the nurses.

Rumor has it that Michael had cancer in his liver. The doctor's report said not to contact his wife. Now the big question is: were Alice and Michael getting a divorce?

Could it be that with Alice being pregnant he didn't want to give her anything else to worry about? Did he think that he could keep it from her until after the baby was born, trying to give her as little stress as he could? Was he thinking he would tell her when the baby was born because he had three years left to live?

That is all the magazine said. It was to be continued tomorrow. I felt numb all over. Everything around me went black.

Chapter 9

"Casey, have you seen Alice since she went on the ride with James?"

"No, I thought she was with you."

"No, Rebecca and James were with me. I can't believe she missed the girls do the egg and spoon."

"That's funny. She was looking forward to watching them. What do you think happened?"

"I don't know. Are the guards at the trailer?"

"No, they are here. Keith, will you go see if she is at the trailer?"

"Yes. I'll be back. If I'm not back in two minutes, then send some help."

"Okay, time starting now."

I hopped on Leo and rode to the trailer. I found Sarge rearing up in the trailer and Midnight backing away from the trailer, trying to break the tie. She was backing up in a funny direction.

Then I saw Alice. She was lying on the ground, face-down in the dirt. A magazine lay by her head.

When I got over to her I called her name, but she didn't move. I hopped off Leo and knelt down next to her; she didn't move. My firefighter training kicked in. I immediately felt for a pulse; she had one. I quickly turned her over, careful not to jostle her. I picked her up and brought her to the bed in her trailer. I was patting her cheeks, trying to get her to wake up. "Alice, honey, wake up. You're okay. "

She started to stir. Outside I heard somebody yelling, "Keith, Alice, where are you?"

I opened the door and found Casey standing out there, looking around. "Casey, come here quick." I held the door long enough for her to see me and start running.

"What happened?" she asked as she walked through the door and saw Alice lying on the bed.

"I don't know. I came back to look for her, and Sarge was going nuts in the trailer. Midnight was trying to break her hold on the trailer. Then I saw Alice lying there face-down and unconscious. This magazine was lying by her head."

"She tried to do too many things at once and overwhelmed herself. Keith you should maybe read this article."

"Is it something I should hear from her? I know how those stories can be misleading."

"Probably, but aren't you curious as to why things keep happening? Why she hid for four years? Why everybody keeps going crazy now that they found her again?"

"I am, but I think it should come from her, not from a magazine."

"You surprise me; most people would have ripped the magazine out of my hands. It is so sweet that you want to hear it from her."

"It's her story to tell, not some magazine. I want her to feel comfortable around me to tell me her secrets." Alice began to stir some more, so Casey and I stopped talking.

"Where am I? What happened?" Alice asked, trying to sit up. I helped her sit up.

"Alice, you are in your trailer, and you fainted over by Midnight. When you didn't show up to watch the girls do egg and spoon I went to look for you. When I got here Sarge was going nuts in the trailer and Midnight was backing away weird so she didn't step on you. She couldn't quite reach you with her nose."

"I missed egg and spoon?"

"Yes."

"I really wanted to see them do it."

"That's why your mom and I got worried when you didn't come to watch."

"What's up now?"

"Ribbon race."

"We have to saddle up. It's ribbon race, and then it's four in a line. We have to get to work." I looked at Casey. Alice must have seen the silent exchange because she said, "What?"

"Are you sure you feel all right?"

"Are you two going to make a big deal out of this? I panicked about something they wrote in the magazine. That's all it was."

"If you feel okay, let's saddle up," Rebecca said.

"Honey, are you sure?" It was the first time Casey spoke since Alice woke up.

"Mom, I'm not like Michael. I didn't pass out because I have low blood sugar and cancer."

"Michael had cancer?" I asked.

"Haven't you read the magazine article? I was pregnant when he was diagnosed, so he didn't tell me. Mom didn't tell me either."

"No, I haven't read the article. I figured that when you were ready to tell me you would want to do it. I want to hear it from you, not some magazine."

"Okay, I'll tell you someday." With that, she turned and walked out of the trailer. She started to calm Sarge down.

We all lined up and ran the pattern. I ran on Sarge. When we got done we went and got Rebecca and the girls. James disappeared after the girls did egg and spoon. He left Dakota there.

"Rebecca, what happened to James?"

"He got a phone call and left. Told me to tell everybody good-bye for him."

"I'm glad he left Dakota. Sarge isn't going to be able to do it. I tried it again. He keeps tripping over his hooves. I'll ride Dakota back and pony Sarge back to the trailer."

"Can I ride with you?" Rebecca asked.

"Sure." When we got out of everybody's earshot, Rebecca spoke up.

"What happened earlier?"

"I found a magazine by Midnight when she whinnied at me. I think Michael's trying to send me a message. I picked up the magazine and read the rest of the article. I got a little panicky over what they said and passed out. Keith found me by Midnight, lying face-down, and carried me to the trailer. That was all that happened."

"Okay, I believe you." We were at the trailer, so I untacked Sarge and put him in the trailer. When we were done we ran back to the arena.

When we got there the horses had two minutes to cool off, and then we went in. Mom on Midnight was first, Keith on Leo was second, I was on Dakota in third, and Rebecca on Ghost was last.

When Mom took off, Keith was having trouble getting Leo to go. "Leo, walk on!" I yelled. Leo took off in a walk. "Run!" I yelled, and Leo took off after Midnight in a dead run. Rebecca and I acted quickly and took off.

When Rebecca hit the last barrel and the timer stopped, we all jumped off our horses. The scoreboard did not have a time. The announcer turned on the microphone and said, "I'm sorry, there seems to be something wrong with the scoreboards. Their time was fifteen seconds." The crowd went wild.

We all hopped back on and rode out of the arena. When we got out I took the lead and motioned for everybody to follow. When I was sure that everyone would follow, I headed to the trailer.

"I thought Leo didn't know commands. I thought only Sarge knew commands," Keith said to me after we all jumped down.

"All the horses know commands. Sarge is the only horse I own that will follow the command if I'm not on him. Like in the barn the other day when I yelled 'rescue' and Sarge came running."

"Okay, I get it now. You took a chance that he would think it was you on him and follow your commands."

"Exactly, now I'm going to get Sarge out of the trailer and try to calm him down. I'm going to go wash out his cut so it doesn't get infected." I opened the trailer, and Sarge came barreling out of the trailer as soon as the door was open wide enough for him to fit through it. I looked to see why Sarge was freaking out, and a million cameras flashed at me. I screamed and caught Sarge. I jumped on, and we ran to the other side of the arena.

I heard Alice scream, so I looked outside. I was just in time to see Alice jump on Sarge and run away.

Then I saw Tyler running to the trailer. I ran to the back end of the trailer and saw all the people standing in there with cameras.

"Call the police," Tyler told me.

"Why?"

"Because they stepped on personal property and scared the wits out of the owner. They are trespassing." Right then Alice rode up on Sarge.

"Don't call the police," she said when she came to a sliding stop.

"But we could have them put in jail for trespassing, and then they won't be able to come near you. They would have to leave you alone."

"No, I said we are not calling the police. Let them out."

Tyler did as she said to do. She must be a tough boss because he didn't say one more word. "Listen up. I will answer five questions of my choice. After that, you will leave me, my family, and friends alone. You are allowed to take only three pictures of me, so make them good. Tyler, I want you on my left. Keith, I want you on my right. If they do not listen, you have the right to cuff them and send them to jail. Question number one."

Everybody shouted at once. "I see I'm going to have to teach you some schoolroom manners again. What your mamas and teachers taught you didn't stick. Raise your hands, and I will call on you." Everybody raised their hands immediately. I picked the person in front of me.

"Why did you go into hiding after the accident?"

"I was hurt. I just lost my husband and baby. I didn't have the strength to face the questions or people taking pictures of me grieving."

"Why did you decide to let us ask you questions now?" somebody blurted out. Tyler looked at me, waiting for the okay. I shook my head.

"I didn't call on the person who just asked that question. Leave now." The person left. I picked the person that filled in that spot.

"Were you and Michael getting a divorce?"

"No!" I picked the guy standing by the trailer.

"Why did Michael keep his cancer secret from you?"

"He kept it from her because she was pregnant and didn't want to put more stress on her. He loved her and the baby. He didn't want her to worry," Mom said as she walked over to us.

"As Mom said, I was very pregnant, and he didn't want to put stress on me." I picked the shortest person there.

"Do you wish he told you?"

"Of course I wish he would have told me. I would have loved to hear it from him, not Mom. I can't blame him for not telling me, because I was very emotional." I picked the tallest person there. "This is the last one."

"Do you think Michael killed your baby?"

"No! Michael loved me and our baby. He would never have let me drive that night, but he was not feeling well. I told him that if he didn't let me drive, I would walk home. He knew that I wasn't kidding, so he let me drive." Keith must have been able to tell that I had enough and I was on the verge of tears. He spoke up.

"That is all for now." He helped me off Sarge. "Tyler, will you tie up Sarge?"

"Sure."

"Thank you." He led me to the trailer.

"Why did they blame Michael for my baby dying?" I mumbled.

"I don't know."

"What killed my baby was all the jostling around from the car going in the ditch and hitting a tree."

"I don't know, honey. I can't read their minds. I can't even give you my opinion because I don't know the story." I said.

"I'm sorry. If you read the magazine, they're pretty close."

"I'll tell you what I told your mom. I want to hear it from you, not some magazine."

"Thank you." The girls came running in the trailer.

"Alice, there's someone here to see you," Caroline said as she took a seat by her daddy.

"Okay, thank you." I walked outside and gasped when I saw who it was. I ran and threw my arms around him. It was Michael's brother, Noah. He didn't look much different after four years.

"How have you been?" he asked when I finally released him.

"Not so good. Have you seen what they have been saying about my husband?"

"That's why I'm here."

"Why?" I was very confused. It must have been all over my face.

"Alice, when Michael found out he had cancer, he came to me. He asked me if he should tell you. I told him to wait. You were already stressed over the baby. The doctors said that the cancer could be passed on to the baby and you wouldn't know until it was too late if the baby had it or not. They would not be able to do chemo or radiation fast enough to save the baby's life. I told him not to tell you everything, especially that it might hurt the baby. He made me promise that if he never got around to it that I would tell you.

"After your mom took him in, he went back in. He had a bunch of other tests done. He found out that not only did he have cancer, he also had a tumor. It was closing in on his heart. He was scheduled for surgery a week after your due date. He said he would not miss the birth of this baby. He loved it too much and wanted to be there with you."

"Why did Michael do it? Why didn't you let him tell me? If I had known I would have treasured all the time I had with him."

"He and I were both scared that you would overdo it if you knew. As far as he knew, he had three years left."

"You're right. I would have overdone it, but we never would have gone to save Midnight."

"Please tell me you don't blame yourself for Michael's death." When I didn't answer, he knew the answer to his question. I could never lie to him. Just like I could never lie to Michael. "Alice, it wasn't your fault. It was bad timing. If it's anybody's fault, it's the cow's. You were trying to do the right thing by saving Midnight. If that farmer would have checked his fence, then that cow wouldn't have been out and you wouldn't have had to swerve."

"Why does everybody keep telling me it's not my fault? It is. If I hadn't seen that horse, we never would have gone. Since I was so pregnant, I never would have gone; but it was a palomino, and I couldn't let her be abused. I told Michael that either he came with me or I was going alone." I was crying. Noah took me in a hug and let me cry into him.

"Alice, it's not your fault or Midnight's. If you want to blame somebody, blame me. If I hadn't told Michael not to tell you about the cancer, you would have known and not gone to see Midnight. You would have been with him."

"It's not your fault. Don't blame yourself for Michael's death. Are you going to come out to the ranch and see Michael's pride and joy later? Come over for supper, since the best cook in the world didn't listen to me and is going to be paying me back by making me a really good supper," I said, laughing a little. He managed a smile.

"Only if I get to see you jump Midnight. Your mom and I have kept in touch over the years. I know you're scared of Midnight and won't go anywhere near her."

"You and my mom have been talking behind my back?"

"Only when she doesn't know what to do with you. I've always loved you like a sister. You know that, right?"

"Of course I do. You know that I still love you like a brother, right?"

"I figured that out when you jumped out of the trailer and threw yourself at me. I think that guy and those two girls are trying to figure out who I am." I walked with Noah over to Keith.

"Keith, this is Noah. Noah, this is Keith, Jane, and Caroline. This is Michael's twin brother. I haven't seen him in four years, and with all the stuff about Michael, he wanted to see how I was doing."

"Nice to meet you," Keith said, shaking hands.

"Nice to meet you, Keith, Jane, Caroline. Girls, do you ride horses?"

"They all do now. The girls wanted to learn, and Keith lost the same bet you did the first time I got you on a horse," I said. Keith looked at Noah.

"You fell for the same trick?" Keith asked.

"The 'how fast can Alice saddle a horse' trick. Michael tried to warn me, but I didn't listen. She can sure saddle a horse fast, can't she? I've never lived it down."

"She saddled that horse in less than two minutes."

"I know. Isn't she amazing?"

"Noah, while you are here, why don't you go watch the rodeo? I'll be up in a little bit. I have to wash out Sarge's cut. Why don't you go talk to Mom, although you probably don't have anything to talk about," I said, changing the subject.

"Okay, but walk with me up there." We started to walk up as the paparazzi figured out who was here. They all ran over at the same time and peppered him with questions.

"Everybody, you have already had your five questions, and Noah is part of the group; so leave him alone, or Tyler will have fun throwing you in jail for trespassing." Everybody turned and ran away from us.

"What was that all about?" Noah asked me.

"They hid in my trailer and scared the living daylights out of me and my horse. I saved them from going to jail, but I had to let Tyler have a little fun. In order to make Tyler happy, I had to give them one warning and let Tyler take over from there. To make them happy, I had to agree to five questions of my choice and they were allowed three pictures."

"You are so mean."

"I know, but that is how I get things done."

"I know that's how you get people on horses, and I'm going out of my way to get you on Midnight."

"Noah, do you think people can send messages from heaven?"

"Yes, I do. Why do you ask?"

"I think Michael is trying to send me a message."

"How?"

"Through Midnight." I saw his mystified look, and I continued to explain. "When I walked down after giving

Keith's friend James his first ride. He screamed like a little girl and decided that he wanted Keith to give him his ride." He started to laugh.

When he could finally breathe, he asked, "How did he end up on top of a horse?"

"He made a bet that I couldn't wash his mouth out with soap by myself." He started laughing again, except harder. "When I came back Midnight whinnied at me, and when I walked over there she put her head in my hand. She let me scratch her head. Then I saw the magazine over there, and I read the article again and finished it. I passed out, and I swear I went to heaven. I could see and talk to Michael like he was right in front of me. He kept saying, 'It's not your fault.'"

"That is an interesting theory. Can I tell your mom this?"

"No."

"Why?"

"She would only freak out and make me go home."

"Fine, I won't tell."

"Thank you. Mom's surrounded by all the guards. Just say your name, and they should open up and let you in."

"Okay, thanks for talking to me."

"Yep. Remember, you owe me a stop for supper tonight."

"I will, if you get up on Midnight."

"Fine, I will, only because I know how much Michael wanted you to see the ranch. I remember how much it meant to him that you were going to finally see it."

"Fine."

"They're setting up jumps. I have to go. Keep everybody distracted. Don't tell anybody what I'm up to."

"Okay, I won't." I took off to go get Midnight. When I got her to the trailer I tacked up Midnight and jumped on. She got a little excited and started to prance. When I got her calmed down we started up for the arena. When I could hear the announcer, I stopped.

"Okay, ladies and gentlemen, I'd like you to look to the back of the arena. Billy the clown is going to do some juggling for us." That was my cue to get to the arena, so when everybody turned to the back of the arena, I came in from the front in the shadows.

The announcer saw that I was in my position, so he started talking again. "Thank you, Billy. Now in the arena I'd like to give a warm welcome to Alice Carlin. She saved this beautiful horse and turned her into a real piece of work." The crowd went wild.

I gave Midnight a good kick, and we went sailing over the first jump. We rounded and headed for the second jump. She started to shy away from it, but I put my hand on her side, so she knew it was okay. She corrected herself and sailed over it. When we landed, we stumbled a little bit. We flipped around to face the third jump in the middle of a stumble. Midnight went down on her front hooves.

I was kicking so hard to get up she wouldn't move. Her back legs started to go down. I got ready to jump off her. "Midnight, up!" I screamed frantically.

Alice surprised us all by riding in on Midnight. The only person who looked like he knew what was going on was Noah.

"Noah, did you know Alice was going to do this?" Casey looked over at Noah, waiting for an answer. Noah just nodded his head.

"Sorry, Casey, I wanted to tell you. But Alice made me promise. She knows all about our phone calls from after her mental meltdowns."

Casey cut him off. "Noah, stop. Keith doesn't know the story yet. Alice isn't ready for Keith to hear it."

"I'm sure he's read the magazines."

"No, I offered the magazine to him, but he turned it down."

"Really?" Noah asked me.

"She will tell me when she is ready. I want to hear it from her, not read it in some magazine. You never know what is true in those magazines."

"All of it is true except for the divorce part. I'm proud of you. Most people would have ripped it right out of Casey's hands in two seconds. Most people would have thought Mom gave me the okay, so it must be okay; she won't care. Are you sure you don't want to read it and find out what all this mess is about?"

"I don't want the magazine." We all watched Alice sail over the first jump; we cheered her on. She went into the second jump and stumbled when she landed. Midnight was not regaining her balance. I looked at Noah.

"Is this part of jumping?" I asked him.

"No, give me your horse." I gave him Leo without thinking twice about it. He jumped on and started running to the fence. The fence was low, so he could jump it. He and Leo sailed over it, and he yelled, "Rescue!" to Alice.

"Midnight, get up." She went down on her hind legs. I glanced over just in time to see Noah jumping the fence on Leo. I heard him yell, "Rescue!" I got ready to jump off and onto Leo, but that did it. Midnight went down. She landed on my leg, but she tried to get up.

Noah jumped off Leo to come and help me get up. I couldn't stand up on my own, so Noah picked me up in his arms. "Are you okay?" he asked as we walked over to Leo.

"My leg hurts. I think I can still move it. It just hurts too much to try."

"She went down on your leg, so it's probably broken."

"Why did she go down? I had just got done riding her. She wasn't limping or favoring any hooves."

"I don't know. She sailed over the first jump fine, and fine on the second jump, but she couldn't land it."

"Is she okay? She wouldn't get up or even try to stop herself from going down."

"I don't know. Two cowboys went to look at her." We walked with Leo right behind us to everybody. When we got to Mom, the guards surrounded us.

"Keith, will you look at her leg and see if it's broken?" Mom asked. Noah must have had some confusion showing in his eyes because Mom quickly started to explain. "Keith is a firefighter. He's the one who pulled Rebecca out of the fire."

"It's not broken, but it's probably sprained pretty good, so stay off of it for a while," Keith said.

"Or it's just that it's my bad leg. What, Noah? You keep looking at me funny."

"Fire?"

"You two didn't talk about Rebecca's apartment going up in flames? Put me down. It doesn't feel right when you hold me. You're Michael's brother, not Michael. Did you tell Michael to stop carrying me around the house when I got pregnant? If you did I'm going to have to hurt you."

"Michael stopped carrying you around the house because you got too fat and he couldn't get his arms around you. It pretty much killed him not to."

"Dang, I had to get pregnant. Life was going good before that happened."

"Shut up, that baby was Michael's pride and joy. Almost as much as that ranch."

"Speaking of ranch, are you coming out tonight? I got on Midnight but didn't get all the way through. Was the deal broken because of it?"

"Are you kidding? Like I would miss a meal cooked by your mother."

"I fell for that trick, didn't I?" When he nodded his head I asked, "What do you want for supper? I'm thinking porter house."

"That sounds good to me."

"Who is cooking this?" Mom asked.

"You are."

"What? I'm only one person."

"A person who didn't listen to me and is the best cook in the world. You owe me. Keith, you and the girls want to join us?"

"Sure."

"Does everybody want porter house?"

"Yes," everybody said at the same time.

"I can't make that many porter houses at the same time that fast."

"Well, it's a good thing you have Mandy to help you."

"Okay, I'm leaving now because all of a sudden I have an abundance of porter houses to make. Did you trash the house when I was gone? If you did you better get in that truck and head home because you have a bunch of people coming over."

"Yep, I did trash the house, and feel free to clean my room."

Noah started laughing. "You never have liked cleaning your room have you?"

"What do you mean?"

"You dated my brother. I saw your room when you were a teenager."

"That was a long time ago, and plus, we could be in there all we wanted. I just had to tell Mom that I was cleaning my room and Michael wanted to help."

"You know we weren't fooled, right? Noah and I had some predictions when we talked all the time," Mom said.

"Bye, Mom. I'm expecting my food done when I get home."

"Don't be so rude, or you won't get any. Bye."

"Bye. Noah, Keith, let's go see what happened to my horse."

"Do you want me to go get Sarge so you can ride him?" Keith asked.

"No, just throw me on Leo." He did what I asked him to do. When I went to make Leo walk, he wouldn't move because Keith was still hanging on to him. "Keith, will you please let go of Leo?"

"Sorry."

"It's okay, trot." Leo went into a smooth little trot.

We got to Midnight, and Keith helped me down. He wouldn't set me down, and it felt so right to be in his arms. "How does she look?" I asked a cowboy. "I don't know what happened."

"I think one of her hooves is cut too short," a tall cowboy said.

"But I haven't had her hooves cut, since…" I trailed off, trying to remember.

"Since?"

"Four weeks ago, and Mom has ridden her a lot since then."

"By the way, these hooves look they were cut right before you came out. The front left hoof is still bleeding. It's the worst job I've seen."

"Tyler, come here." He came running. "Did you have somebody by the trailer all day long?"

"Yes, ma'am."

"How many people, and were they allowed to go to the bathroom and leave the trailers unattended?"

"One person, and I never thought of the bathroom thing. I put Josh there."

"Okay, thank you." I knew that Josh left, because he wasn't there when I walked back to the trailer. But how many times did he leave and how long? "Okay, boys, step away; and, Keith, set me down." All of them stepped away, but Keith didn't set me down. He was staring into the stands.

"Keith." I got his attention and started struggling out of his arms. He tightened his arms on me. "Will you please set me down?"

"Are you sure?" he asked, very careful not to let any expression in his voice. His voice didn't give him away, but his eyes did. His eyes were all hazy, like he was scared of what Midnight might do to me.

"Keith, I've broken my leg before. I can manage just fine." He set me down, and I wanted to crawl right back into his arms, but I had to take care of Midnight. "Boys, back away farther. The girls need their room to bond." All the boys backed away. "Noah, I need your help."

"Why do you need my help?"

"You look a lot like Michael, and Midnight loved him. I need you to rub down her neck. I don't know what she will do because the first time I touched her without Michael she got hurt."

"I get your point. She might shy away from you."

"Exactly. Now will you rub her down?" He walked over to Midnight and started rubbing her down. While he was rubbing her down, he was talking in a soothing voice. My eyes started to mist.

"Why are you crying?"

"You look exactly like Michael did that day we saved her. He sat there talking and rubbing her because the sight of me freaked her out."

"I'm sorry, Alice. Why did I have to look so much like my brother?"

"Because you were his identical twin."

"That's true. Why did you pick him, considering we look so much alike?"

"Because he was sweet and you were wild and crazy."

"I was not wild and crazy!"

"Really? Racing snowmobiles, jumping dirt bikes, and partying all night. May I add coming to my house violently sick?"

"Fine, you win. I was wild."

"And crazy."

"Fine, what do you want me to do now?"

"Just keep petting her while I walk up to her." He kept petting her, and I walked slowly toward her. When I made it to her, I started petting her too. "It's okay. I won't hurt you. It's okay." She lifted her head and whinnied.

"I don't think you need to worry about that."

"I don't think so either. Go stand with the rest of the guys."

"Okay." He went and joined the other guys.

⁓

"She is bossy, isn't she?" Noah said to me.

"It looks like she is used to being bossy." I was watching Alice very carefully, and by the recent events around Midnight, I was waiting for her to freak out.

"A girl has to be bossy if she's going to make it in the modeling world," Noah said, taking me out of my thoughts.

"Is she thinking about going back into modeling?"

"I don't know. I haven't really talked to her since the accident."

"Why?"

"'Cause, I knew that if I did I would have to tell her about Michael having cancer. It isn't easy for me 'cause I kind of feel it's my fault."

"Okay let's drop the subject 'cause I'm totally lost."

"That's right. You don't know the story. I'm glad you want to hear it from her. Even though I'm not her brother-in-law anymore, I still love her like a sister," he said with a little warning in his voice.

"That's sweet." I got a big scowl from that. "I think she loves you like a brother too."

"I know she does. That's why I had to come see how she's doing." I glanced back to Alice. She had Midnight by the halter and was rubbing underneath it.

"Why is she doing that?" I asked Noah.

"I don't know. It might have been something Michael did when he first saw her."

"She blames herself for Michael's death, doesn't she?"

"You want me to answer that?"

"Yes."

"Why do you ask?"

"Because she cries so much when she talks about him. She was crying so hard when she read the magazine that they started to pack up and go home."

"Really?"

I nodded.

"I didn't realize it was that bad. She does blame herself, but it wasn't her fault."

"I've picked that up between you and Casey. She better tell me what's going on soon, or I will have to read the magazines."

"How much do you like her?"

"Like who?"

"Don't play dumb with me. You know who I'm talking about. Alice." I looked up at her; she was pulling on the reins and yelling something at Midnight. Nobody else was looking at her. They were watching me. "If you don't take her, then you're nuts. I'd take her in a minute," somebody said in my ear.

"Keith, Noah, will you get my trailer and stop gossiping. Noah, I know you are pinning down Keith for answers to stupid questions."

"Okay, and for the record, we weren't gossiping," Noah said, sounding annoyed. Probably because she nailed it right on the nose. "We are not little schoolgirls. We're not you and Rebecca." I started to snicker and didn't realize Rebecca was standing right behind me. She smacked me on the top of the head.

"Ouch!" I complained.

"He's definitely a little girl," Rebecca said to Alice.

"Noah is just as much. Noah, you want to dance around the ring later?" Alice asked, sounding a little persuasive. Noah quickly shook his head and started running to the trailers. I watched him run to the trailers with his tail between his legs until I realized I was the only one left to dance around with Alice. I looked at her and back at Noah and ran for the trailer too. I heard everybody laughing behind me until Alice asked if they wanted to dance around. The laughing cut off immediately.

When we got to the trailer, we made sure that everything was shut tight, made sure Sarge would be okay in there with the trailer in motion, and jumped in the truck.

"You know, you never answered my question earlier."

"What question?"

"You know, about Alice."

"Did you ask a question about how much I like her?"

"Duh. I think she likes you."

"I like her too."

"How much do you like her?"

"I don't want to answer that question. We better get going if Alice wants this trailer. We're already in trouble with all those cowboys that watched us run away like cowards."

"That's true, but if they give me too much trouble, I do have a few years of practice fighting Alice."

"You have actually had to fight against her?"

"Sure. How do you think I got her to concentrate on me instead of her husband?"

"Was it that difficult? As far as I see, all you have to do is ride up on a horse."

"Yes, it was that difficult. Your idea would have worked if Michael wouldn't have been a professional rider."

"Professional rider?"

"Yes, how do you think Alice got her perfect riding stance?" By now we were at the arena. Alice saw the trailer and started getting Midnight up again. They started walking slowly to the trailer. Noah jumped out of the truck, and I followed suit. Noah went and got Midnight from Alice, and I started opening the trailer door. I opened the door, and Sarge came bursting out the door. He ran straight at Alice. She started screaming orders at him.

"Sarge, down. Walk." When he didn't obey she said some words I could tell she didn't want to say: "Sarge, at ease. Do it for Michael and Haley! Hoe!" Sarge stopped immediately. "Good boy." All the cowboys started to clap. Alice walked around to Sarge's left side and went to his hind leg. "How are you doing, buddy?" Sarge gave a loud whinny and shook. Alice jumped on bareback and they started to go around the track.

The announcer started to speak. "Alice is going around on Sarge. It's the old team again!" They sailed over the first three jumps perfectly. Then they stopped. Alice looked over at Noah and nodded her head at him. He nodded his head right back at her.

Alice hopped off Sarge and went to the fifth jump and set it as high as it would go. They walked over to the side of the arena. When she finally made it to the side of the arena, she looked at Sarge. He walked over to her, and she put two barrels in front of him and three poles on his back. She helped steady the poles and told Sarge to start walking. When Sarge would take a step, he would push the barrels closer to the jumps.

I looked over and was going to ask Noah a question, but he was gone. I looked out into the arena, and Noah was out there. Alice looked right at me and waved me over. When I got over there I asked her, "What are you doing?"

"Sarge seems to be doing okay, so I'm making the jumps more difficult for him. When I had to take Midnight, I had them set the jumps down to her jumping height, the standard."

"You're setting it up for Sarge's ability to jump."

"No, I'm setting it up so everybody has an equal chance at winning. Now I need another strong man to help put these up." Noah and I each grabbed a side and put it up. "That's good. Thank you." She hopped up on Sarge, and we ran out of the arena.

When we were out of the arena, I asked Noah, "How high are those jumps?"

"They should be about five and a half feet tall."

"Why did she have to put every thing else out there?"

"It's going to make it more difficult for Sarge." Alice came up to the jump, and I saw what he meant. Sarge had to jump early and slowly get higher until he passed over the five-and-a-half-foot jump.

"That was amazing!"

"Yes, it was. She and Michael used to hold rodeos for the people they used to compete against."

"Really, they were that competitive?"

"Yes, they traveled all around the world. If she didn't have to do something for her modeling career."

"Was she very popular in her modeling career?"

"Yes. She almost always had something to do. I don't think she wants to get into it again."

"Why?"

"Because they were never together in public. They would go together but get separated by the paparazzi or fans."

"I guess that would drive anybody nuts." Alice came riding bareback up to the trailer, and a cowboy opened the trailer for her.

Chapter 10

"Are you ready to go to my place?" Alice asked as she walked over to us. "Where are Rebecca and the girls?"

"I think they went for a trail ride."

"I bet they went to the old hideout." Alice looked at Noah, and they both started to laugh. They took off running. I walked after them.

"What was that look shared between you two a couple minutes ago?"

"The place we are going is where Noah tried to kiss me while Michael and I were going out. Michael saw what he was going to do, and I was his girl, so he beat his brother up in a fist fight."

"He did kick my butt, didn't he?"

"He kicked your butt so hard you limped around for a week."

"Yeah, Mom grounded him for a week."

"I remember, 'cause Michael and I couldn't go out for Valentine's Day."

"That's right. Sorry. I shouldn't have been such a baby."

"You were such a baby, and I really didn't care. I kind of thought it was funny. Plus, Michael and I did meet that night. We met at midnight in my garden."

"That's so sweet. If I would have seen him, I would have knocked him out and went to meet you," Noah said.

"Sorry, but I never really thought you were that cute."

"That really hurts the ego."

"Good, now let your ego take this. Michael was a whole lot better kisser than you."

"Okay, let me get this straight. You loved her, and she was going out with your brother?" I asked.

"That's correct. Noah, do you remember how to get there?"

"Duh. That was my favorite spot."

"Good, I'm going the way Michael and I used to go, and you two are going the right way."

"No, your mom would kill me if I left your side."

"Then let her kill you." And with that she started walking to the woods.

"Come on, let's go."

"Aren't we going to follow her?"

"No."

"Why not?"

"Hey, lover boy, nobody is allowed back there except Michael and Alice. I've tried to follow them, but I can never figure it out."

"Has Rebecca been back there?"

"Has Rebecca what?" somebody asked from behind me. I flipped around, and Rebecca and the girls were right behind me. My expression must have been surprised because the girls started laughing. "I'm sorry. I didn't mean to scare you."

"It's fine. I was wondering if Alice has ever taken you through her and Michael's passage."

"No, how did you find out about that?"

"Alice went that way, and Noah started telling me about it."

"Noah, should we go watch for old times' sake?"

"Okay, Keith, you and the girls coming too?"

"Girls, you want to go?"

"Yeah!" both girls yelled. Noah grabbed Jane, and I grabbed Caroline. We all went in the fort.

I was surprised at what it looked like. It was like woods surrounded by brick walls. "Watch your step. That's where I broke my arm," Noah said. We got over to the middle when Rebecca and Noah hooked arms and started singing "Strangers."

"Why are you singing that song?" They didn't stop singing, but Alice came bouncing from tree to tree, singing the same song. When she got to the last tree she jumped and landed right in Rebecca and Noah's arms.

"It isn't right without him. I'll just have to find someone new to share the secret passage with." Rebecca and Noah pretty much attacked her. She ran and hid behind me. "Not either of you. It will be with my husband, if I ever find a guy who will be good to me, and if I ever decide to get married. If I'm ever going to find somebody, I better keep my eyes open and stop hiding. I need to get out of this open show by the looks on your faces. I just gave away some information I didn't want to." We all started to walk out together. "Caroline, do you want to ride with me?"

"Yeah!"

"Jane, do you want to ride with Rebecca?"

"Yeah!"

"Keith and Noah, you're riding together."

"What?" Noah said.

"You were not smart enough to bring Leo, so you can ride together. The only horses we got are from Rebecca and the girl's ride." Rebecca and I looked at each other and nodded. We held the girls tight and made the horses do a full-out run. We heard Keith and Noah yelling at us.

When we got to the trailer we all hopped off and started to untack horses. Keith and Noah still hadn't made it back by the time we put the horses in the trailer, so we went into the air-conditioned trailer. "So have you got anybody in mind who might get to learn the passage?" Rebecca asked.

"I'm not answering that question."

"It's Keith, isn't it?"

"Maybe, maybe not."

"Does the guy have any kids?"

"Rebecca, stop asking questions. I don't want to play that game."

"Fine, but only because the guys are coming." Noah untacked Twilight and put her in the trailer.

"What did you do while you were waiting for us?"

"Rebecca wanted to play twenty questions, and I said no. She didn't get the meaning of *no* very quickly."

"Does Rebecca ever get the meaning of *no* very quickly?"

"Don't be mean!" Rebecca yelled.

"Okay, everybody hop in a vehicle!" I yelled, so everybody could hear me.

"Can I ride with you?" Jane asked as she and Caroline came running over.

"Me too?" Caroline asked in a sweet voice.

"It's fine by me if it's fine by your daddy." They ran over to Keith and asked him.

"Can we ride with Alice?" Jane asked him.

"What did Alice say?" he asked them, looking at me. I nodded.

"She said we could," Caroline said.

"Okay, we'll ride with Alice." When everybody was in the truck, we started for the house.

"How long until you expect your mom to have supper done?"

"I don't know. I was going to have everybody go to the dance room over the barn."

"Dance room?"

"Yes, you sound surprised."

"I am. Why do you have a dance room over the barn?"

"Because it wouldn't fit in the house, and I wanted Michael and our families to have a dance for our wedding."

"Why didn't you have a dance like normal people in a public dance room?"

"You're forgetting who I am. We didn't want a bunch of paparazzi at our dance like they were at the wedding."

"I guess that makes sense." We pulled up to the house ten minutes later. We got out and pulled the girls out of the backseat. We walked over to Rebecca and Noah.

"How many acres is this?" Noah asked.

"Ask my mom. Rebecca, should we show them to the dance floor?"

"Yeah."

"Do we get to dance?" Caroline asked.

"Sure you can."

"Yeah!"

I led the way to the barn. Keith stopped by stall number nine.

"Alice, what's wrong with this horse?" Keith asked. I walked over to the stall, and Koda was rolling, and when she got up she was biting at her flanks and sweating. After she was up for a minute, she laid down again.

"Rebecca, run to the tack room and grab a bunch of lead ropes. Keith and Noah, keep the girls out of stall." I grabbed the lead rope by her stall door and ran to clip it on her halter. "Koda, get up." I had the rope around my midsection and threw all my weight into the opposite direction of her. I couldn't make her get up.

Rebecca came back with a handful of lead ropes. "What's wrong with her?"

"I think she has colic. Rebecca, will you go call the vet? Her number is on the board in my office."

"Isn't it the normal number?"

"No, I got a new vet that lives closer I want to try."

I hooked another lead rope to her halter. "Keith, stand with the girls. Noah, come here. I need your help." When Noah was in the stall, I slammed the door shut and tied the lead rope to the door.

"What do you want me to do?"

"You're going to use your muscles and help me get Koda on her feet." I gave him a rope, and he started to pull. When we finally got her up, I dropped my rope and braced myself so she wouldn't go down again. "Get her walking to the automatic water." He pulled her over, and I pushed her head into the water.

The vet got there just as she started to drink. "It looks like she's doing okay." At the sound of her voice, Koda looked up. "What happened?"

"We were going up to the dance floor when Keith saw her and asked what was wrong with her. So I checked her, and she had all the signs of colic. When I tried to get her up, she wouldn't, so that confirmed my diagnosis."

"I wish all my patients' owners knew horses this well."

"I save abused animals, not just take them so I can abuse them some more. I've had her for two years, and she still is scared of a lot of people. Will you look at Midnight while you're here?"

"Sure, what's wrong with her?"

"We were at the open show, and I'm guessing one of my fans thought it would be nice to cut her hooves for me. We went over our first jump just fine and went over the second jump fine, but we couldn't land it. She went down and had trouble getting up. When we got her up she was limping a little bit."

"Let's go take a look." We unloaded Midnight from the trailer and brought her to her stall.

When we got down to eye level with her legs, I saw her back one was swollen. "What do you think?"

"Her back leg is definitely swollen. I want to take some x-rays."

"Okay, we'll let you work. If you need anything, just go up those stairs."

"Thanks." We all left the veterinarian alone and went up to the dance floor.

⁓

Alice let the veterinarian do her job and led us up to the dance floor. When we got up there I couldn't believe my eyes. It was huge and looked like it was decorated for a ball. "Why is it so dressed up?" I asked her.

"This is what our wedding reception looked like. Michael didn't want to take down the decorations till Noah saw it, and to laugh in your face and tell Noah I was his while you danced with me. We were going to throw another wedding reception so everybody could be here."

"That sounds like something Michael would do to me. I wish I could have been here. Why did you never take down the decorations after Michael's death?"

"Do you want the truth?"

"Yes."

"I thought if I took them down it would seem like Michael was really gone forever." Tears were starting to stream down her face.

"Alice, you know Michael isn't coming back," Noah said carefully, trying not to upset her more.

"I know. I haven't been up here since Michael's death."

"Alice, Michael wouldn't want you to be unhappy. He would want you to get on with your life and live it to the fullest."

"I know."

"You can start by going on a date."

"With who, you?"

"No, that would just be wrong."

"Alice, would you go on a date with me?" I asked, still standing in the doorway.

"Yes!"

Casey came up right at that moment, and by the smile on her face she had been listening. "Supper is ready."

The vet came flying up the stairs. She said, "Alice, I need to talk to you." Alice went flying down the stairs after her.

"So, Casey, how much of that conversation did you get?" I asked her.

"Just the ending."

"How much of the ending? By the way you were smiling, I think I know what part." Noah started to laugh and gave Casey a hug.

"Well, Noah, we are getting pretty good at predicting things."

"What's that supposed to mean?" I asked.

"Noah and I always predicted that Alice would get her first date since her husband died when we reunited for the first time. Every year since my daughter's husband died she gets really depressed. Keith, today is that day, and she hasn't cried once because of what day it is."

"Hey, what's wrong with Midnight?" I asked the doctor as we ran down the stairs.

"Her left hind leg is broken at the ankle."

"What can we do for her?"

"I can set it, but there is a chance she could be lame when it heals. We can try to do a surgery on it."

"Okay, where will I need to send her?"

"I can take her to my office and do it there."

"Perfect, when do you want her?"

"Tomorrow morning. I can do it around eight thirty."

"I'll have her there by eight, or is that too early?"

"Perfect." She left, and I made sure all the stalls were locked. I went to the house and found everybody looking at photo albums.

"What are you looking at?" I asked everybody. Caroline and Jane were laughing. "Girls, what's so funny?" I walked over to stand behind them.

"You were really fat," Caroline stated.

"Caroline, that's not nice to say," Keith scolded.

"It's okay. It's a picture of when I was seven months pregnant. Mom, why are all these out of my room?"

"Don't you know what day it is? I'm keeping the tradition alive."

"It can't be five years, can it?"

"It was five years ago today." I looked down and saw a picture of the funeral in the photo album the girls had. I looked at Noah, and he must have seen the panic in my eyes because he got up and tried to catch me before I ran to my room. He wasn't quick enough, though, and he got air instead of me.

When I was in my room I locked my door and collapsed on my bed.

Everybody just froze from the outburst of Alice. "That didn't go as I expected it to," Casey mumbled. I looked at Noah. He turned and walked the way Alice had fled. I followed him. Rebecca hugged Casey, trying to comfort her.

When we got to Alice's room, Noah tried to open the door. It wouldn't open. "Alice, open the door please. Your mom is really worried about you," Noah said. She wouldn't open the door. Noah turned to me. "You try to get it to open."

"Do you want me to break it down or try to get her to open it?"

"Try to get her to open it, but if that doesn't work, use your break-down-the-door thing."

"Okay. Alice, will you please open the door so we can talk? The girls want to give you hugs." At the mention of girls, Jane and Caroline shot their heads up. I waved them over. When I looked back over at Noah, he was smiling like a fool. "What?"

"Try the door." I grabbed the handle and twisted it. She had unlocked the door. "She opened it for you but wouldn't open it for me. I'm hurt."

"Wrong. She opened it for the girls."

"Believe what you want to believe."

"I will." I looked at the girls. "Go give Alice a hug." The girls ran in and jumped on the bed.

"What's wrong, Alice?"

"Nothing. Are you ready to eat?"

"Yes," Jane said. They all came out and went to the dining room, and I followed behind, so she couldn't run back to her room.

"Sorry, Mom. The date caught me off guard."

"It's okay. Let's eat." We all sat down and said grace.

"So, girls, did you have fun today?" Rebecca asked.

"Yes, my favorite was when I was riding with you and we got back before Daddy and Noah," Jane said.

"Why was that your favorite?" I asked.

"Because of Daddy's face."

"My favorite was doing egg and spoon," Caroline said.

"Sorry I missed egg and spoon, girls. Can I ask you to do a favor for me?" They both nodded, so I continued, "Since I missed it, I was wondering if you would show me in the arena." I caught Mom's look and quickly added, "After supper." The girls started shoveling food in their mouths. I had to laugh. "Slow down, girls. I'm a slow eater, so it's going to be a while."

When everyone was done, all the girls took the dishes to the kitchen. We put them in the sink and went back to join the men.

All the girls went outside at the same time because the men were deep in a conversation. "So, Caroline, should we go for a ride later? The ride I'm thinking about you would have to ride with an adult."

"Yeah!"

"What about you, Jane?"

"Yeah!"

"Rebecca, Mom, would you like to go?"

"Sure," Mom said.

"What trail are we taking?" Rebecca asked.

"What trail is the most fun to run through at night?" Mom asked.

"Are you talking about the cabin trail?" Rebecca asked, still confused.

"Yes."

"Is Keith going to be able to make that trail? He is pretty new at riding."

"I will let Keith decide if he wants to ride with somebody or by himself."

"Are you going to tell him what trail we're going to go on?" Rebecca asked.

"No, what's the point? He isn't going to know what I'm talking about. Noah will pretty much talk him into riding with somebody when he finds out what trail I'm talking about."

"Why is that?" Rebecca asked.

"'Cause like you, Michael and I took him out. Noah was pretty new at riding. This was around the time he was trying to get my eyes off his brother and on him. Let's just say Michael and I took off in a dead run and Noah fell behind. He couldn't find his way there." I was saddling horses as I talked. Mom was in the arena with the girls taking down the jumps.

"What did you guys do?"

"Well, Michael and I sat on the log and watched a bunch of coyotes run. When they were gone, we talked for about four hours. Then we decided that Noah was lost and we had to go find him."

"How long was he out there?"

"About five hours. Michael was grounded for two weeks because he was supposed to look out for his brother. The girls should be ready to ride. Will you go get the men. Pull them out by their ears if you have to." I started laughing because knowing Rebecca, she would.

~

Rebecca came barging into the house and told us to get our butts to the barn. When we didn't move she took us by the ear and dragged us out of the house. "Alice gave me permission," she said.

"Okay, I'll follow. Will you ... will you let go of my ear?" I begged. She let go, and I heard all the laughing. Alice, Casey, and the girls were standing in the barn entrance.

"Did they give you any trouble?" Alice yelled to Rebecca.

"Not once I got hold of their ears!" she yelled back, and Alice started laughing harder.

"Why did you give her permission?" I asked Alice when we got to them.

"Because it's fun to see full-grown men get pulled out by a little woman."

"Very funny."

"Ready to watch the girls?"

"Let's go."

"Okay, see who can last the longest." They took off in a walk. Jane's egg was starting to shake after one minute. Twilight got scared and jumped. Caroline tried to steady her egg but failed. The egg dropped. Jane's egg went down right after Caroline's did. They rode over. "You were great, both of you." Their faces just beamed with joy.

"Can we go for our ride now?" Jane asked.

"Yes, we can."

"What ride?" Noah asked, sounding a little scared.

"The one you fear most. Keith, I can saddle a horse for you or you can ride behind somebody."

"Keith, if I were you, I'd ride with somebody," Noah said.

"Why?"

"Because the first time I went out on that trail was with Michael and Alice."

"What did they do?"

"They took off in a dead run and I got left behind. They left me out there for five hours."

"What were they doing?"

"Who knows?"

"We sat there and talked, if you have to know," Alice said from right behind me. I whirled around and she smiled. "Have you decided what you want to do? The girls would like to go now."

"Knowing that information, I'll ride with somebody."

"Who are you riding with?"

"I'll ride with you."

She laughed and said, "Suit yourself."

When she left I looked at Noah. He was shaking his head.

"Why are you shaking your head?"

"Because you are in for a ride of your life." Alice came in and dragged us out before I could ask why.

Noah and Keith were deep in conversation and didn't look like they were going to be done soon. I walked in there and broke up the conversation. They looked a little worried. "Are you ready, Noah?"

"Yes."

"Everybody ready?" When everybody nodded, I let Keith climb on behind me. "Are you ready?" I asked him.

"Let's go."

"Yah!" Sarge took off in a dead run. Keith said something, but I didn't understand it. Sarge rounded the first corner, and Keith's arms tightened around my waist. I slowed down. "Keith, will you please loosen your grip around my waist?"

"Sure, sorry." When he loosened his grip I urged Sarge into a run again. His grip tightened when he felt our speed increase.

When we got to the end, I jumped off Sarge and found the switch on the electrical pole to turn on all the lights down the trail. Keith grumbled, "Sure, now you turn on the lights." Louder he said, "Why do you keep rubbing your waist?" I hadn't realized I was.

"Because Mr. Firefighter had a death grip around it. Why did you pick me to ride with? You know I don't take it slow."

"This explains why Noah said I was in for the ride of my life. I picked you because you are probably the most experienced rider I know and the lightest. I was trying to make it easier for the horse."

"Little tip of advice. Don't make it easier for the horse on the way back. Look over there."

"What am I looking at?"

"That's where you will see the others in about five minutes."

"Why so long?"

"If you didn't notice, I love this trail and run all the way through it. They have to walk or trot all the way through until the lights come on. The only horses that know the trail well enough to run through it are Ghost and Sarge. Rebecca is too scared to take him through it that fast."

"If you love the trail, why do you run through it?"

"Because I like this view more."

We sat in silence for a long time. Something moved in the bush, and we jumped. "Stay here," Alice commanded me. I did exactly as she said and stayed put.

Moments later she came back. She had a gun. "Where did you get that?"

"Michael and I put a shed out here when we first saw the coyotes."

"That explains it!"

"We never really told anybody about it 'cause we were still in high school. We would sneak out and meet here. Michael always knew he would get the ranch, so he didn't feel the need to ask anyone."

"You two pretty much had your future planed out for you, didn't you?"

"Yes, Michael and I both loved horses, so we new it would be a horse ranch. We both loved each other and wanted to get married. We were going to elope at the age of sixteen, but we decided that we would wait because our parents would kill us."

"Yes, they would have," somebody said from behind us. We both jumped. We hadn't heard anybody come up behind us. We turned around at the same time, and Casey was standing right there. Behind her were Rebecca, Noah, and the girls, all laughing.

"I'll ride with Rebecca on the way home," I said to Alice. "If you will take Jane with you."

"Of course I'll take Jane with me, but only if she wants to run. If she doesn't want to run, I'll put her with Noah."

"Okay." I walked over to Rebecca. "You have a new passenger."

"Why?"

"Because Alice doesn't know how not to run when she gets on a horse."

"Why did you pick her if you didn't want to go fast? Alice never rides slow."

"I forgot that detail. Alice and going fast when you can see is not so bad, but when you are in the pitch dark, it's a little scary."

"Yeah it is." Alice was walking over.

Keith and Rebecca were talking, and Jane was staring out where the coyotes were running across the field. "Jane, do you like to run in the dark?" Her little eyes lit up.

"Yeah, can I ride in the dark like you and Daddy did?"

"Sure." I helped her down, and Keith jumped up.

"Take it slow with him. He's kind of a chicken," I told

Rebecca, and she started laughing. "You can start heading back if you want. Mom just started home because she is getting tired."

"Okay, are you ready, Keith?"

"Yeah, for a nice, slow ride."

"The slowest you're going to get is a trot around the corners and a gallop on the straight shots."

"Works with me. I'll have light."

"Alice is right. You are a chicken."

"Okay, you have five minutes, starting now." They took off. Noah saw everybody leaving and took off too. "You want to sit on that log over there?" I asked Jane.

"Sure, how long do we get to sit here?"

"About five minutes. Do you want some water?"

"Yes, please." We walked back to the shed and got bottles of water.

"Here you go, honey."

"Thank you."

"You're welcome. Let's go watch the sun set." We watched the sun set for a while "We have to go. Your daddy's probably wondering where you are."

"How long have we been sitting here?"

"Maybe ten minutes. Let's head back to the ranch." We jumped on Sarge, and I killed the lights. "Are you ready?" I asked Jane when it was completely dark.

"Yeah!" We took off speeding through the woods.

Alice sent everybody back so we could ride with the light and she would ride in the dark. Rebecca was a lot nicer to ride with than Alice.

When we got back we unsaddled the horses. We turned them out and went back to the barn to put the tack in the right spot. Rebecca loaded me up with a saddle and three bridles. "The saddle goes in here," she said. When we put the saddles away we started for a different spot. "The bridles and halters go in her office."

We came up to the door, and she opened it and went in. Alice had pictures of her, Sarge, Michael, and another horse at a rodeo plastered on one wall. On another there were before and after pictures of horses.

"They are some of the horses she has saved," Rebecca said, catching me staring.

"How many has she saved?"

"I don't know. That's a question Alice would know off the top of her head. She is proud of the horses she has saved."

"How does she get people to hand over their horses?"

"She asks them if she can take them off their hands. Normally, abusive owners don't want their horses, so they just give them up. If that doesn't work, she offers them money that they can't refuse. Money is not an issue."

"I guess that would work."

"Speaking of Alice, how much do you like her?"

"Noah asked me the same question. Why?"

"Because of the way you look at her, and we love her and don't want to see her hurt again. She was devastated when Michael and her baby died."

"I don't want to hurt her, and I like her a lot."

"You should ask her out on a date."

"I did that earlier."

"Well, what did she say?"

"What do you think she said?"

"Yes." I nodded and she squealed.

"She's finally moving on with her life."

"Shouldn't they be back by now?" I asked her, trying to get on a different subject. I didn't want to discuss my feelings about Alice with Rebecca. Especially since I didn't know exactly how I felt about her.

"Yes, they should." We walked to the barn exit. Nobody was in the barn or coming up to the barn. We sat there for two minutes.

"Should we go look for them?"

"No, they probably lost track of time watching the sun set. Watch the horses and be quiet."

"Why?"

"Be quiet and watch."

I pushed Sarge as fast as he could go. Jane sat in front of me, giggling. I slowed to a walk. I asked Jane, "Are you okay?"

"Yes, can we go fast again?"

"Sure, but I have to sing. I can't sing and go as fast as we were going."

"Okay." I urged Sarge into a gallop and started singing "All the Pretty Little Ponies."

The horses all started to whinny at the same time. When they whinnied it had a rhythm to it. It sounded so familiar, but I couldn't place it.

"Does that mean they are coming?" I asked Rebecca.

"Yes. Do you know what song it is?"

"I know it, but I can't place the name."

"It's 'All the Pretty Little Ponies.' When she wants to know how close to home she is she sings that and the horses answer her."

"My mom used to sing that song."

"Really? Where do your parents live?"

"They live here about fifteen miles out of town."

"That's nice. You can drop the girls off at their house if you get sick of them."

"I can, but I never get sick of them."

"Where do they go when you have a date?"

"I haven't had a date since my wife died."

"Really? You two are perfect for each other."

"What's that supposed to mean?"

"Just that you and her both haven't dated since your husband or wife died. What will the girls think?"

"I think they will be fine with it. They get to go over to James's house."

"Why his house?"

"James made a promise to me, because he thinks I have no social life, that if I get a girlfriend he will watch the girls.

"So now that he butted into your social life, you're going to take him up on his promise. Nice!"

Chapter 11

I could hear the horses echoing me, so I knew I was close to the house. I slowed Sarge down to a trot.

We came around the last corner. Keith and Rebecca were in a deep conversation. "Should we try to sneak up on them?" I asked Jane quietly. She nodded. "We have to be very quiet." She nodded again. "Sarge, sneaky."

Sarge stepped very carefully. "Hang on tight, okay?" Jane nodded and gripped the horn harder. Sarge kept creeping until we were seven feet away from Keith and Rebecca. I whispered, "Now!" I quickly grabbed Jane really tight.

Sarge jumped and whinnied loud. He started to do bunny hops. Rebecca screamed and ran for the protection of the barn, and Keith ran after her. "Down, Sarge," I said. When they were in the barn, Jane started laughing hysterically and I joined her.

We trotted into the barn laughing so hard that we were crying. Keith and Rebecca just stared at us. Rebecca finally got it. "That was so mean."

"I thought it was hilarious."

"That was you?" Keith asked.

"Yes, and you are a chicken."

"Michael and she always did that to me if they didn't like my boyfriend. They used to come at you from both sides."

Mom and Noah came running into the barn.

"What's wrong? We heard somebody scream," Noah asked. Jane and I started laughing again. Mom got it right away.

"I thought I heard some whinnying out here. You haven't done that since Rebecca's last boyfriend. What was his name?"

"Jesse. He had gorgeous eyes."

"He dumped you by a text message."

"Okay, that was dumb, but he didn't know how to break up with me in person."

"What did you do to her?" Noah asked, still so confused.

"What I did to you and Lauren when you were dating."

"Wait, she did it to both of you?" Keith asked. They both nodded.

"I didn't approve of them, so I scared them off."

"That is so mean." Keith said.

"I know. But it worked."

"It sure did. I'm heading home," Noah said.

"I'm going to bed," Mom said.

"Bye, Noah. Night, Mom."

"Alice, I'm going upstairs to the apartment if you need me." Rebecca said.

"Why are you going to the apartment?"

"Because that's where I'm sleeping."

"Really? That's news to me. I thought that you were sleeping in the room next to mine."

"Okay, I'm going to the house then."

"Night, see you later."

"Bye, girls."

"Bye, Rebecca," They said together.

When Rebecca finally disappeared Keith said, "Girls, we should probably go."

"Do we have to?" Caroline asked.

"I don't want to go," Jane stated.

"It's time to get in the truck."

"I'll have one of my guards bring you back to your vehicle."

"Thank you. What time do you want me to pick you up?"

"Pick me up?"

"For our date."

"I don't know. Where are we going?"

"That's a surprise."

"Please, nowhere public."

"Fine, nowhere public. Pick you up at five?"

"Sounds good."

"Bye, Alice!" The girls yelled and Keith walked out.

We all got in the car and drove to the hospital to get our car. When we started going, my cell phone rang. It was James. "Hi, what do you need?"

"Where are you? You're not at the rodeo."

"We are just leaving Alice's ranch. Why?"

"I was looking at a piece of paper when I heard there was a fire. Are you on call?"

"No, where was it?"

"Four miles out of town. I thought Alice lived a little ways out of town?"

"She does." I turned to the driver. "Turn around. I need to go back."

"Okay," he said.

"Thanks, James," I said into the phone, "Talk to you later." I hung up before he could say anything else.

"Are you okay?" the driver asked, seeing the expression on my face. If it was on Alice's property, then I would have to question her about who would set fire to her property. That is if it wasn't a fire started by nature.

"There was a fire four miles out of town, and I think it might be Alice's property."

⁓

When Keith left I hollered, "Okay, he's gone. You can come out of hiding." Noah, Rebecca, and Mom came out from different directions of the barn. "So, tomorrow at five?" Rebecca asked.

"Yes, and if you eavesdrop you might hear things you don't want to hear."

"What are you going to wear?" Mom asked.

"I don't know yet. Are you going to ask a question, Noah?"

"No." Just then I heard a truck pull up to the barn and a truck door slam. "I do have a question. Are you expecting anyone?"

"No. Let's go find out who it is." We all walked out to

the truck. It was Keith. "Keith, what are you doing here? I thought you left?"

"I did. How far out of town does your land start?"

"Four miles. Why?"

"I think there might be a fire in one of your pastures."

"Come on. Everybody in. Grab flashlights." Everybody got in, and we headed to the field. "Keith, how did you find out so fast after you left?"

"James called. I guess he was looking for me to find out if I was on call."

"Are you on call?"

"No, but being one of the top firefighters on our staff, I have to make my rounds and question people. Since I was out and moving, I thought I would make my round tonight, so I asked where it was. He said it was four miles out of town."

"So you thought of my ranch." We could see where the fire was. "That is not my property. The property line is this side of the woods about four feet out."

"That's good, because I would hate having to question you."

"Do you think somebody thought it was my land and is trying to get back at me for disappearing?"

"Maybe, if you look at it that way."

"Well, I'll keep my eyes open and let everybody know if I see anything. Let's head back. Do you have to stay and help them?"

"No. They can handle it." Everybody jumped in.

"I thought everybody went to bed," Keith said as everybody got out of the tuck and headed for the barn.

"That's what they wanted me to think."

"So that they can call in the party over what they heard eavesdropping." I started giggling.

"You nailed exactly what they are doing."

"I kind of knew what they were doing when I saw Noah and Rebecca sticking their heads out to hear better."

"I knew exactly what they were doing when they all left at the same time and in different directions."

"So did they play twenty questions on you?"

"Yes. Did James play it on you when he called?"

"No, I hung up before he could. I'm expecting a phone call back from him in five minutes."

"Why five minutes?"

"Because it's routine. If he is telling me about a girl he's going to set me up with on a blind date, I hang up. He waits five minutes, hoping I cool off, then he calls back. If I keep ignoring him, he keeps it up all night."

"Turn your cell phone off."

"I've done that, but then he calls the house phone."

"That sucks."

"Tell me about it. What kind of questions did they ask you?"

"What I'm going to wear and stuff like that."

"What did you say?"

"I don't know."

"You don't know what you said?"

"I said, 'I don't know.'"

"Okay, I get it. That's what you told them."

"Rebecca, stop eavesdropping. I see your hair."

"Noah, I see you too."

"Mom, give up. I know you're listening too. Come out and join the conversation."

Rebecca was the first to come out.

Rebecca asked, "Where are you going to take her? I'm playing twenty questions on Keith. Anybody want to join?" Mom and Noah came running over. Just then Keith's phone rang.

"Five minutes are up. Let James join in on twenty questions." Keith flipped open the phone and listened for a few seconds. "Hold on one second, and you can join the fun," Keith said into the phone. He put James on speaker phone.

"Hi, James, it's Rebecca. We're playing twenty questions on Keith. You want to join?"

"Yes. When are you going on a date?"

"Tomorrow at five, and I think you're going to be on kid duty," I said.

"That's right. You have promises to fulfill," Keith said.

"But I have a date tomorrow."

"You have to cancel it."

"Nobody is canceling dates. I'm watching the girls tomorrow. I talked it over with the girls when we got home." Casey said.

"Sorry, but James has promises to fulfill, and he will. He owes me."

"Back to my question. Where are you taking her?" Rebecca asked Keith.

"Let me answer this one," I said. Keith shrugged, and I continued, "Wherever he wants to take me. We're not telling you because we are grown-ups and can go on a date without killing each other." After about ten more questions,

I looked at Keith and asked, "Keith, isn't it past the girls' bedtime?"

"Yes."

"No, it's not," Mom stated.

"Let me guess. They said it was at eleven o'clock." When mom nodded Keith continued. "For lying, it is now eight o'clock tomorrow night. It was originally nine." Everybody started laughing.

"What a typical child," I said just as Keith started shaking his head.

"Bye. No more playing twenty questions on Alice or me. You had your chance," Keith said, getting into the truck after putting the girls into it.

When they were gone, I said, "I'm going to bed."

When we got to the vehicle, the girls were sleeping. Instead of waking them I lifted them from the truck to the van and strapped them in. On the way home my cell phone rang again. I didn't need to look. I knew how it was. "Hello, James," I said into the phone.

"I'm not James."

"Alice?"

"Who else would it be? You never told me what I'm supposed to wear."

"Why do I have to pick out what you wear?"

"Because I don't know where we're going. Should I dress up? Or jeans?"

"You can wear jeans, or you can dress up."

"Fine, I'll dress up." She hung up. We were just pulling up to the house as I closed the phone.

"Girls, we're home." I shook them awake.

"Daddy, where are we, and where is Alice?" Jane asked.

"We're at home and Alice is at her house. Come on, let's go to bed." Caroline wasn't waking up, so I carried her into the house to her bed. I helped Jane take off her shoes and climb into bed. "Night, honey."

"Night, Daddy." I gave her a kiss and went to my room.

I caught myself thinking about where I'd take Alice on our date tomorrow and what she was going to wear. I could picture her wearing that red dress again.

Chapter 12

After I got off the phone with Keith, I was even more confused about what I should wear.

I came to the conclusion that I was wearing the blue summer dress with my blue high heels and laid them out. Then I went to bed. When I finally fell asleep, I caught myself dreaming about what would happen tomorrow on our date.

There was a knock on my door the next morning. "Honey, are you awake?"

"Yeah, just woke up."

"Are you going today?"

"Going where?"

"To church with me."

"Yeah, how long do I have to get ready?"

"About forty minutes."

"Thanks for waking me up, Mom."

"You're welcome. Forty minutes." She turned and walked out of the room.

I went to the bathroom and got ready. When I was showered and had my make-up on, I went to the closet. I pulled out the red dress I wore the first day Keith was out here.

When I was done getting ready, I ran to the car, where Mom was waiting. "Are you ready?" I asked Mom. She was staring out the garage window. "Mom what's wrong?" I asked when she didn't answer my first question.

"Don't you have to bring Midnight in this morning?"

"Let me make a quick phone call." I grabbed my cell phone and dialed the vet's number. She answered on the first ring, "Hello."

"Hey, it's Alice. Can I change Midnight's appointment to this afternoon?"

"Sure, how about two this afternoon?"

"That's perfect."

"Okay, see you this afternoon."

"Bye." I hung up the phone and jumped in the car. "Midnight will be in at two o'clock." Mom nodded and backed the car out of the garage.

When I woke this morning I was surprised at how tired I still was. I fell back to sleep for half an hour and then got dressed for church.

I went into the girls' room and started waking up Caroline. I shook her lightly, and she started to stir. Caroline was harder to wake up than Jane was. "Jane, wake up," I said from across the room. She didn't wake up, so I walked over and shook her. She woke up immediately.

"Daddy, what day is it?"

"It's Sunday, and you need to get ready for church."

"Okay, I'll go shower."

"I'll lay your outfit on your bed."

"Can I pick out my outfit for church?"

"Sure, as long as I get to approve it."

"Okay."

"Go shower, and I'll get your sister out of bed." She ran out of the room so she didn't have to wake up her sister. "Caroline, wake up."

"I'm tired; can I sleep longer?"

"No, you have to get up for church."

"Is Jane in the shower?"

"Yes, she should be out in five minutes, so get your outfit." When she didn't move, I made it more threatening. "If you don't pick out your outfit right now, I'll pick it out for you." That did it. She jumped out of bed and ran for her closet.

I walked to the kitchen after I was sure she wouldn't go back to sleep. I started getting out the cereal and bowls when Jane came in. "Daddy, what's for breakfast?"

"Cereal. You look nice." She was wearing a red summer dress. It looked like the one Alice was wearing the first day we were out there. She had one of her old necklaces on. She got it when she was three years old. "Come here, Jane." When she came over I undid her necklace and took her to my wife's old jewelry box. I pulled out a red necklace and put it on her.

"Daddy, was that Mommy's?"

"Yes, Daddy gave it to Mommy the year she was pregnant with you."

"Why?"

"Because Daddy loved giving your mommy presents." Caroline came running in.

"Why does Jane get to wear one of mommy's necklaces?"

"You both can if you have my permission. Would you like to wear one to church?"

"Can I?"

"Of course you can. This one will match your outfit." It was a blue flower. She was wearing a blue summer dress with flowers on it. "We need to go," I said, looking at the clock.

We all ran to the garage and got in the car. When everybody was buckled, I backed out of the garage and started for the church. When we got there, James was waiting for us.

"You're running a little late."

"I know."

"Hi, Keith, girls, James," somebody said from behind us. I'd know the voice from anywhere. It was Alice. I spun around. "Looks like we're not the only ones running late."

Jane tugged on my coat. "Yes, Jane?"

"Can we sit with Alice and Casey? I don't want to sit with the little kids today."

"If it's okay with Alice and Casey, it's okay with me."

"It's fine with me," Alice said.

"Me too," Casey seconded.

"Okay, you can sit with them, but be good. We have to go."

"Go. I've got the girls. See you later," Alice said.

"Thanks." James and I turned and ran to the back doors to meet up with the choir. When we were inside we slowed to a walk.

"So you and Alice?" James whispered.

"Don't start," I whispered back forcefully.

"Fine."

When we got to the church, James, Keith, and the girls were standing outside the church talking. It looked as though Keith and the girls had just gotten there. When Mom and I got to them, we got the girls to come sit with us through the church service.

When Keith and James went to go sit by the choir, we went to find a pew. When we got in the doors, everyone turned to look at us. We just kept walking. We found a pew with two people in it. It was big enough so that we could all fit in it.

When we sat down, the people around us gave me their bulletins. "Will you sign this?" the lady in the pew asked.

"Sure." I grabbed a pen out of my purse and started signing autographs. "No more autographs," I said as the minister walked out to the podium. Everybody sat down in their pews and listened to the sermon.

The sermon was on if you follow God, there will always be light at the other end of the tunnel. The girls were very into the sermon. They pulled out notebooks and took notes on the sermon. When it was time to sing, they stood up with the congregation and sang.

Church was over at ten o'clock. We walked down to the breakfast hall to meet with Keith and James. We beat them there, so we got a plate and sat down to wait for them.

"I like your dress, Jane. It looks like mine. I like yours too, Caroline. I have one that looks like that too."

"I wanted to look like you," Jane said. "Daddy said I could wear whatever I wanted as long as he approved."

"And he approved?"

"Yes, he did. Except for the necklace she was wearing, but we took care of that," somebody said from behind. I turned around.

"About time you got here."

"Funny, we were waiting for you," Keith said.

"Well, you found us and we were talking, so go get your food." Keith and James left to go retrieve their food. "Jane, I'm flattered that you want to dress like me."

"What does flattered mean?"

"It means to make someone feel pleased or honored. Caroline, I was going to wear my dress like that tonight." Keith and James were sitting down at the table.

"That's good to know," Keith said.

"So are you going to tell me where you are taking me tonight?"

"No."

"Why not?"

"Because it is a surprise."

"I hate surprises," I grumbled under my breath. It must have been louder than I thought because Mom started to talk.

"You love surprises. Michael used to give you surprises all the time."

"Be quiet, Mom."

"No."

"Fine, then keep reminding me to get the latest gossip magazines."

"Fine, I'll shut up."

"Thank you." We sat in quiet for the rest of the time.

When everybody finished eating, we all got up to leave."

Mom and I stopped at the gas station and got the latest gossip magazine. "Don't you read that until we can read it together," Mom told me.

"Can I look at the pictures?"

"No! We will look together. Throw it in the back if it's going to tempt you." I threw the magazine in the back. "What are you wearing tonight on your date?"

"What I'm wearing now. Can we please not start up questions now?" When we got home from church we changed into jeans and t-shirts and got Midnight to the vet. After we returned home we changed into summer dresses and headed into town for groceries.

We were heading home from town when Mom said, "Fine, I won't ask you questions about your date, but can I ask you questions about the girls?"

I rolled my eyes.

"Fine, what do you want to ask me?"

"How do you like the girls?"

"I love the girls. I look at them and see their daddy. I see what my baby could have been like and love them more."

"Do you think you could love them like your own?"

"Yes, I could. Why do you ask?" She shrugged. "Mom, don't start thinking about weddings."

"I wasn't."

"If you are thinking about weddings, then I will have to hurt you."

"I thought you liked Keith?"

"I do, but I haven't even been on a date with him."

"You could count all the times he was out here and being at the fair."

"No. A date is where two people go out in public together and have dinner and maybe a movie, and don't count tonight as a date."

"Why?"

"Because we're not going someplace public."

"I thought it was a surprise."

"It is, but I asked him to not take me someplace public."

"Yes, but you didn't consider your mom working with him did you?"

"You wouldn't dare, and you don't know his number."

"Yes, but I bet that Rebecca would love to see you go some place public too. His number is on her phone, as I understand."

"She wouldn't dare give you his number. Besides, I can take her phone before you get to it and delete his number."

"That would work, but I know you too well. I got the number before this conversation."

⁓

After breakfast I took the girls home to change out of their church outfits. When we got home, Caroline went to change and Jane went to watch television. I started making lunch.

Caroline came out dressed in blue jeans and a t-shirt. "Jane, will you please change?" Jane waited for a commercial and ran to her room to change. She didn't want to miss any of her show.

"Daddy, what's for lunch?" Caroline asked.

"Grilled cheese sandwiches. Does that sound good? It's something quick and easy to fill your hungry little belly."

"Yeah, that's my favorite."

Jane came running into the room. "What are we eating?"

"Grilled cheese sandwiches." Her show came on, and she ran back to the couch.

"Daddy, are you and Alice going out for supper?" Caroline asked.

"Yes, is that okay?"

"I like Alice. Are we going to Grandma's house?"

"No, you're going to James's house."

"Are we spending the night?"

"I bet you could if you asked him."

"Okay, I'll ask him." We all sat down and had a quick lunch. "Can we go to James's house now?"

My cell phone rang.

"Let me answer the phone first." I grabbed my phone. "Hello?"

"Hi, Keith, it's Casey."

"Hi, Casey. What can I do for you?"

"You need to take Alice somewhere public for dinner tonight."

"She told me nowhere public."

"I know what she told you. She would rather go someplace public."

"Where should I take her?"

"Take her to Grandma's. Dress nice, and I'll have her wear her blue summer dress. Rebecca and I will be there, and I will get the bill, so you have a reason to do this and put up with my crabby daughter."

"What should I wear?"

"Nice jeans and a t-shirt. I don't care. Bye." She hung up before I could say another word. We all sat down and started watching the show Jane was watching and lost track of time. When I looked at the clock it read two thirty.

"Let's go, girls."

We got in the van and started for James's house. The girls were out of the vehicle before I even had my seatbelt off. Instead of knocking on the door and waiting for him to answer it, they ran in. James just let them go and came out to meet me. "Do you have time for coffee?" he asked.

"Sure."

"So have you decided where you're taking her?"

"Yes, to Grandma's," I said, sitting down in a kitchen chair.

"So you decided to take her someplace public?"

"No, it's more like Casey did for me. She called me before we left my house."

"What did she say?"

"That I was supposed to take her to Grandma's and she would foot the bill."

"Nice. You take a pretty lady out on a date and her mom picks up the bill." I glanced at the clock. I had an hour and a half until I had to pick up Alice.

"Bye, James."

"You're leaving already?"

"Yeah, that's why I said bye." I was out the door and in the van before he had time to blink.

Chapter 13

I walked into the living room after spending the afternoon in my room. Mom quietly hung up the phone, but before she did that it looked like she sent a text message.

Rebecca came running into the room and blocked my exit. "What's going on?" I asked.

"You need to change, whether you like it or not."

"Why do I have to change, Mom?"

"Because I told Keith that I would get you in your blue summer dress."

"Why do I need to wear my blue summer dress?"

"Because Keith's taking you to Grandma's."

"You did not do what I think you did, did you?"

"Yes, I did."

"Fine, I'm going to my room to change." Nobody moved. "What?" I turned to Rebecca for an explanation.

"I'm doing your hair and fingernails, and your mom is doing your makeup and toenails."

"Fine, I'm going to get tortured." I walked slowly to my room. "What blue summer dress am I supposed to be wearing?"

"The one that was on your bed will work."

"Let me guess, the shoes I wore for my wedding are the ones I'll be wearing tonight?"

"How did you know?"

"Because this is the outfit I wore on the plane to my honeymoon spot."

"I suppose this is like déjà vu for you."

"Not really. I don't have the excitement that I did walking down the aisle."

"Fine, you don't have to wear the shoes."

"I'll wear the shoes." Once I was in the dress they pushed me into a chair in the middle of the room. "Why am I sitting in the middle of my room instead of in front of a mirror?"

"Because you don't get to look until you're done."

"That is so mean."

"I know, but that is the way it's going to be," Rebecca said. I knew she was right. I tortured her all the time before I got married, so I sucked it up. I let them torture me without a fight.

True to her words, when Rebecca was done with my hair she started giving me a French manicure. When Mom finished doing my makeup, she moved to my toes.

When they were both done they helped me up without letting me smudge anything and helped me to the mirrors. My hair was pulled up into a part bun, and they waved what was lying out of the bun. It was like I had it at my wedding, but my bangs were not curled and left out of the bun.

"What do you think?" Mom asked.

"It's almost the same as my wedding. I could have saved lots of money if I had you do my hair."

We all turned to stare out the window when we heard a car pull up.

On the way to Alice's I was surprised to see how excited I felt. I felt like I was sixteen again, going on a date with the hottest girl in school. I went over the conversations we could have while eating.

When I pulled to a stop I saw Casey and Rebecca standing on the deck. I got out and walked over to them. "You're taking her to Grandma's right?" Rebecca asked. I nodded.

I kept looking at Casey, and it looked like she was trying to determine whether or not she would present her daughter to me. "You came dressed like I wanted you to," Casey said.

"I'm glad you approve."

"The reservation is under Keith and Alice. We are on the other side of the restaurant."

"So you can still see us?"

"Exactly, so if you don't treat her right, we can intervene and beat you up for it."

"You won't have to." We heard somebody walking in the hallway. We all turned to see her.

When Keith pulled up, Mom and Rebecca ran out to the deck. They left me to search for my hidden shoes.

I finally found them and was heading outside when I heard Mom talking. I stood there in silence as I tried to listen to them. It must have been the end of the conversation because they stopped talking when I was close enough to hear what they were saying.

I stepped out and they all turned to look at me. Mom and Rebecca gave me a smile that was obviously a satisfaction smile. Keith just stared. "Mom, Rebecca, stay home. I'm a grown-up and can take care of myself." I knew they wouldn't listen, but I had to try. They did exactly what I thought they would do and shook their heads.

Keith and I looked at each other and headed for the car. When I looked back, I saw Mom and Rebecca running into the house. My guess would be to get dressed.

When we got to the restaurant, Keith told them our names and we were led to the back of the restaurant. All the tables were empty, except one that held an abundance of candles on it. "How much do you think Mom is paying them to seat nobody back here and give us the best service? I also bet she is paying them to let nobody near this spot," I said when we were seated.

"I don't know, but I know they will be sitting right there." He pointed across the room.

"Where are the girls tonight?"

"With James. You knew they were going there."

"That's right. How did dropping them off go?"

"The same as always. They jumped out of the car before I had my seatbelt unbuckled and were running into his house without knocking. It's his own fault. He feeds them candy."

I started giggling. "That sounds like me when I was little."

"Tell me about when you were a child."

"I grew up around here and had braces. The kids called me brace face, train tracks, and geek."

"I'm so sorry."

"It's okay."

Alice and I were doing well for our first date, I thought. We seemed to have a million conversations we could start. It seemed as though we could talk forever and never repeat one thing. It was going well until she asked me about my childhood.

What should I tell her? Tell her that I grew up in a trailer park and my parents beat me? That the only way to get out of my world was to stay late at school and study Indian names? I could tell her the truth, or I could tell her I grew up with the sweetest parents in the world, which was partly true. I came to the conclusion to tell her the truth. "When I was a little I lived in a trailer park with my biological parents. I would go to school with bruises because my parents would hit me when they got in fights. Finally social services came and took me. I would cry for days. Finally, two days later, I made a friend and called her Bala." Alice interrupted me.

"What does Bala mean?"

"Bala is a nine-year-old girl." When she nodded I continued. "We were playing in the park when I saw a bunch of grown-ups walking toward us. Bala asked me what I would call them, and I said Rati, for the women, Rajkumar, for the man." I saw the confusion in her face, so I hurried to explain. "Rati means most beautiful lady, and Rajkumar means prince. Anyway, we watched them for a while, and then Bala started telling me how she got there. Her parents were killed in a car accident, and she missed her horses. Her stud's name was Spirit Warrior. And her pregnant mare was Paco. The people that were there stopped and really started looking at me. The directors started telling them my story. Rati was crying by the end. The director told me to get up and go put my things in a bag. I didn't understand that I was getting up because I was getting adopted. They put me in the car and started introductions. They told me I was going home with them, and they were my new mommy and daddy. I cried and said, 'Don't hit me,' all the way home. When we got there I stopped bawling and saw that I had a room to myself. I love them to death now."

"That is so sad." I could see the tears glistening in her eyes. When she realized I was watching her, she looked away so I couldn't see her tears.

"I thought about not telling you, but you told me the truth about your childhood. It was only fair to tell you the truth." Our food came, so we quickly ate.

"Let's get out of here before Mom and Rebecca get here. It will drive them nuts and keep them off my case for a week."

"Okay. Where do you want to go?"

"Let's go see James and the girls."

"Good, you can tell James I took you out in public and kept him off my back."

"Why would I do that?"

"Because I would be forever grateful."

"Fine, I will, and as soon as we step outside one camera will be getting photos considering they followed us here. I saw them trying to get a picture earlier."

"Well, let's sneak out the back because your mom and Rebecca just showed up." We quickly ran out the back door, and true to her words, cameras flashed.

When we got to the vehicle we started laughing. "How long do you think they will sit there?" Keith asked me.

"Long enough to eat."

"Did you drop Midnight off this morning?"

"No, I dropped her off after church. She was a little jumpy at first, but they calmed her down." We pulled into somebody's driveway. "Where are we?"

"James's house."

"He lives here by himself? This house is huge."

"Him and his dog. He gets lonely, so the girls are here all the time."

"What's his dog's name?"

"It was my dog before I got married, so it had an Indian name, Ayasha."

"Does that mean high one?"

"No it means little one. The girls can't say it, so they call her little one."

"Why didn't you take her home for the girls after their mom died?"

"Because we couldn't have pets in the house we were renting, and playing with Ayasha reminds me of my late wife too much. We got Ayasha during third year that we dated each other. We were still in high school, so Mom said we could keep her there at the farm until we got married."

"Where did you live before where you live now?"

"I lived in my college dorm, and then when we got married we rented a small house by her mom's and the college."

"Do you still keep in touch with her parents?"

"Yeah, the girls normally go there one weekend every two months." I saw Jane look through the window and yell something over her shoulder.

"We've been spotted." I nodded toward the window and started to get out. Keith got out too.

James was out the door before we had made it to the deck. "What are you doing here?"

"Alice wanted to see the girls and take them to the park."

"Before you two get into a big argument, let me say this. Keith was a gentleman and he took me to a great public restaurant. Now that that's settled, can I take the girls to the park now? James, you are welcome to come with us and bring Ayasha."

"How do you know my dog?" James asked.

"If I get this right, it's Keith's dog." James looked at Keith and raised his eyebrows. Keith just shook his head and called, "Girls!"

The girls came racing through the house with Ayasha on their heels. When they saw it was Keith, the girls said, "Sit, stay." When the dog did as it was told, they ran to Keith. They gave each other hugs and then gave me a hug.

Keith looked at Ayasha and gave her a nod. The dog came barreling through the doors and knocked James over. James came up talking angrily, but not one swear word came out of his mouth. Keith hugged the dog and played with her for a while, and then we all joined in.

We played for half an hour before I finally asked if they wanted to go to the park. We all jumped up and Caroline grabbed Ayasha's leash. We headed for the park, Alice and I hand in hand, the girls in front of us with Ayasha, and James behind us probably taking in everything we did.

Alice started talking pulling me out of my thoughts. "I'm planning the next date. A piece of advice. Drop the girls off at Grandma's house and plan on them spending the night. Make sure you come in old blue jeans."

"Do I get to know what we're doing?" When she shook her head, I knew it was payback. "Is this going to be payback for tonight?"

"Yes, and payback sucks. Be prepared, because I might get Mom, Rebecca, and James in on it with me."

"Now I'm scared." I ran up behind the girls and grabbed Ayasha's leash. "I'm taking Ayasha for a run!" I yelled over my shoulder.

"Not without me!" Alice yelled and started running after me. We ran around the park four times, almost two miles. I was starting to get tired, so I started going toward where James was sitting."

"Hey, firefighter, you getting tuckered out?"

"Yes."

"Fine. Poor little baby." She ran past me and jumped on a swing. I went and sat by James.

"She looks like she has a lot more energy than you do."

"Shut up. She feels good now that her leg doesn't constantly bother her."

"Where did you really take her?"

"If you look at the magazines tomorrow, you will find out."

"That's not fair. I won't get the paper till tomorrow."

"James, I think what Keith's trying to say is what you don't know won't kill you," the lady on the next bench said. We both looked over at her. After about two minutes I realized that she was the paramedic from the office. "You finally got a girl."

"Yes, both of you shut up and leave me alone." I walked over to where Alice sat on the swings.

When we got done with our run, Keith went to sit with James. I went to go swing with the girls. When the girls ran to play on the jungle gym, I looked over at Keith. He was sitting with James, talking to another girl. She looked vaguely familiar. He got up and started walking over to me. "How late do you want to stay?" he asked me as he sat down on the swing next to me.

"It doesn't matter to me. I don't work tomorrow."

"Where do you work?"

"Considering I don't get paid, I don't actually work there. I volunteer three days a week at the school."

"That's cool."

"Who were you talking to? She looks really familiar."

"That's Naomi. She is a paramedic on the first-responders team."

"She was one of the paramedics in my ambulance at my accident." I knew he wanted more information on that subject, but I didn't give it to him, and he didn't press for more.

"When you are ready to go home, let me know."

"I'll go when the girls are ready to go."

"The girls are staying at James's house."

"You didn't want them to come home?"

"No, because James feeds them an abundance of candy and pop. They come home wired full of energy because they have a sugar high and don't go to bed till one, two in the morning. I decided it was time for James to learn his lesson."

"You are almost as mean as me."

"I'm learning it from you."

"In that case, let's head to my house."

"The kids and James won't see us if you want to be sneaky again."

"Let's sneak out of here, then." We quietly ran to the bushes, but we forgot about one thing: the dog. She started barking. When James went over to go see what was wrong with her, we made a run for it.

Chapter 14

After we made it to the truck, we looked behind us. James and the girls were running up the sidewalk. I looked over at Alice, and she nodded. We backed out and left.

About five minutes later my cell phone rang. We looked at each other again. She held out her hand, so I gave her my phone. "Hello?" she said into the phone and listened. "We waved. It didn't look like the girls were done playing, and it didn't look like you were done flirting with Naomi either." She listened for a while and then laughed. "Yeah, James, that's all we were going for! Have fun with the girls tonight. Bye." She clicked the phone shut and shook her head.

"What?" I asked, confused.

"James is so dumb."

"Why?"

"He says he wasn't flirting with Naomi."

"I didn't think he was, but I wasn't watching them."

"I was, and he was so flirting." I changed the subject before we started to argue about it. "Are you going to come in and face twenty questions with me, or did you want to go?"

"I'll face twenty questions with you, but I don't think they will ask them with me there."

"That's true." We pulled up to her house and jumped out at the same time. Alice looked out at the barn then busted out into a dead run toward it. She stopped at the barn entrance and grabbed Sarge and a bunch of halters. "Open the gate when the horses come running." She took off in a run again to the gate. She must have seen the confusion in my face because she yelled, "Fire!" and pointed over to the west pasture.

I grabbed my cell phone and called in my team. I ran and threw open the gate for the horses then ran to my vehicle. I grabbed my gear and started running toward the fire.

After I had all the halters on horses and were getting them out to safety, I saw Keith running toward the fire with all his gear on. "Keith, stop!" I yelled frantically, but he didn't hear me.

I tore out the gates to get fire extinguishers. I caught up to Keith, and he took one then told me to go back and get to safety. I listened but didn't get to safety. If the fire continued it would hit the barn. I grabbed a hose and started spraying down the barn. When I was done with that I jumped on Sarge and started rounding up the horses and put them in the pasture on the east side. I ran to the barn and put the horses that were left in there in the round pen.

Mom and Rebecca must not have been home, because if they were, they would have come out to help. Mom would have jumped on Dakota, and Rebecca would have jumped on Ghost.

I thought I heard somebody coming down the driveway, so I turned to see who it was. It was Mom and Rebecca, followed by a bunch of paparazzi. I grabbed Dakota and Ghost and ran to Mom and Rebecca. They jumped on, and we ran behind the barn where all the horses were freaking out. I flung the gate open, and the horses all started running toward safety. I took Sarge to the side, and Rebecca took another side. Mom took the back. I had the pleasure of all their eyes growing wide at the sight of all the horses running right in front of them and then the pleasure of seeing that they were so shocked they didn't get any pictures. We ran back to the barn. "What is going on?" Rebecca asked. Mom figured it out by just looking at me. I was staring at the west pasture.

"Honey, the barn will be fine," Mom said.

"What is going on?" Rebecca asked, growing impatient.

"Fire in the west pasture," I said.

"The ranch will be fine," Mom said.

"I'm not worried about the ranch," I stated.

"He's a firefighter. Alice, he will be fine."

"You really like him, don't you?" Mom asked. I could only nod. My throat was so clogged with emotions I couldn't talk. The fire was moving closer to the barn, so I started to evacuate the last of the horses in the round pen.

"Let's move them to the pasture in the east. I have all the other horses there."

"Let's move, cowgirls," Mom said. We all took off running. We got all the horses into the pasture and started riding back.

Keith was standing by the barn shaking his head when I rode up with Mom and Rebecca right behind me. "You don't listen very well, do you?"

"No, I don't. If that fire had spread and got out of hand, all my horses could have been injured or killed."

"So you put your life in danger?"

"Yes, Keith, they are part of my family. When one of my horses dies, a piece of me dies with them. I have a bunch that are getting old and not doing well. I promised that I would take care of them and prevent them from getting hurt. If keeping my promise means I have to endanger my life, then so be it." Mom and Rebecca hadn't said anything in this whole conversation, but Keith thought they should.

"You all should have gone for safety."

"I have signed a few contracts, and so has Rebecca. We pledged our lives to these horses, and we will keep our promises, even if it kills us," Mom said.

"Keith, if you don't understand the love I have for my horses, then you don't know me. If you don't know me, then get off my property."

"I get you. I just didn't understand how much you loved the horses."

"I think whoever is setting these fires is out to get me."

"That's what I think too, but I'm going to pretend that I didn't hear that."

"Why?"

"Because I would have to take you to my office and interrogate you."

"You don't want to do that?" Rebecca asked.

"No, I would rather do that on a date and without an audience."

"Speaking of date, where did you go after you ate?" Mom asked. I looked at Keith and gave him the okay to leave if he wanted to. He just shook his head and answered the questions Mom and Rebecca dished at him.

"We went to see the girls and ran around the park."

"What time did you leave the restaurant?" Rebecca asked.

"We left right after you walked in the door."

"You didn't sneak by us?"

"No, we used the back doors."

"Why did you go see the girls?" Mom asked. This time I answered.

"I wanted to see the girls. I love them like they are my own. I see them and see how my little girl could have been." Changing the subject, I said, "I think I need to do an interview on why I hid away for four years and why I don't care if people know where I'm at now."

"I think that could be a bad idea," Keith stated.

"Why?"

"If these fires are getting started by somebody, it could be because you are the hottest topic right now and they aren't."

"Fine, you should probably go call James. We didn't exactly give him the appropriate good-bye or cooperate on the phone."

"What do you mean we didn't give him the proper good-bye?" Rebecca asked.

"We were at the park, and James was flirting with Naomi, and the girls were playing. We got up and snuck away. That is, until Keith's dog noticed that we were leaving without her and started barking. We decided to run and got in the truck to leave."

"You didn't say bye to the girls?" Mom asked.

"No, James can have fun putting them to bed," Keith said. "Bye. I'll call you tomorrow."

"Okay, I'll tell you when to meet me next."

When Keith was gone, I went to my room and fell asleep.

I wondered if Alice got peppered with more questions after I left. Did she let the horses back into the other side of the pasture that had the fire, or did she leave them all together? Was somebody trying to hurt her? What would it be like to kiss her? I was dumbfounded at the way my thoughts were working. *Why am I wondering about what it would be like to kiss her? I can't be. What would the girls think?*

I stirred my thoughts to a different topic with a lot of work. I wondered how James was doing with the girls. I wondered how James would take it if I brought Ayasha home. *Would the girls like that? They seem to love Ayasha when I drop them off at James's house.*

When I pulled in my driveway, I realized Naomi was sitting in front of my house on the hood of her car. When I got out, she came to meet me. "Hey, Keith, why did you and your girlfriend run from the park?"

"Because she wanted to go home and we didn't want to play twenty questions with you or James. Are you on call tonight?"

"Yeah why?"

"Did you hear the call about a fire five miles out of town?"

"Yeah, but by the time my team started to leave they radioed and said they didn't need us."

"That was her place. Her ranch. It had seventy-five horses that she saved from abusive owners in one area.

Instead of taking my warning to get to safety, she made sure all the horses were safe."

"It bugs you that she didn't listen to you, doesn't it?"

"Not really. It just showed me she cares about things. I admire her for that. What did you come over here for?"

"I came over to see if James called you. Something about how he gave each of the girls three cans of pop and went through two bags of Skittles." I started laughing.

"He's going to learn his lesson yet."

"What lesson?"

"That you don't put a bunch of sugar in kids before they go to bed. Jane will have to get up and pee twice, and Caroline will get sick and spend the night in the bathroom."

"You're right. You have to give them four cans of pop and four bags of sour gummy worms."

"Remind me to never let you babysit for my kids."

"Only if you get James to go on a date with me."

"I'll do it. Tomorrow, meet me at work and tell me where and when."

"Bye, Keith. See you at work tomorrow." When she was gone I walked into the house laughing. James would pay for everything he had done.

I collapsed on my bed and fell asleep immediately. I started dreaming about Alice. *How would I propose to her, if I proposed to her? How would the girls take it? Would they be the flower girls or bridesmaids?*

Chapter 15

When I woke up I saw Mom and Rebecca staring at me. "What?"

"Why did you go to bed without talking to us?" Mom asked.

"If you didn't notice, I was getting seventy-five horses to safety from a fire. I think I have a right to be tired."

"She does have a right to be tired," Rebecca said.

"Thank you. Now can I please go back to sleep?"

"Not if you want to read this with us." That did it. I was up. Mom handed me the magazine, and it flipped open to the right page. I looked at Mom, and she looked away. "What's in here you don't want me to see?"

"I don't want you to see the article on Keith."

"What's it about?"

"How his wife died and where he grew up."

"I know about all that."

"Well, let's read this article," Rebecca said.

Three days ago Alice Carlin let us ask a couple questions. We asked her if she and Michael were getting a divorce at the time of the accident. She had a strict answer: "No!"

We asked her why she hid for four years. Her answer was, "I was hurt. I had just lost my husband and baby. I didn't want people taking pictures of me grieving." In my opinion, Alice was mad at her husband for losing their baby and not living forever. She didn't want us to see that she wasn't grieving. She was angry.

We asked her why she was talking to us now. She sent the guy away because he didn't raise his hand and get called on.

I think she is talking now because she has found a man she can't leave. I think she's dating a man named Keith. They have been caught hanging out at the rodeo and at the park. She wanted him to stand by her during the questioning.

"Why did Michael keep his cancer secret from you?" somebody asked her.

The response came from Alice's mom, Casey: "Alice was very pregnant, and Michael did not want to worry her. She was already stressed about the baby."

Alice replied, "You heard what my mom just said. Michael loved me so much. He didn't want to put any more stress on me."

"Do you wish Michael would have told you about his cancer?" somebody else asked.

"Of course I do. I would have loved to hear it from him and not from my mom. I can understand why he didn't tell me. I was very pregnant and emotional."

The last question she let us ask was, "Do you think Michael killed your baby?"

Her answer again was a strict, "No! Michael would never have let me drive that night, but he wasn't feeling well. I told him that if he didn't let me drive I would walk all the way home. He knew that I was dead serious, so he let me drive."

The real question is, is Alice the one to blame for her baby's death?

To be continued.

"Well that was boring," Rebecca said to break the silence.

"It's only boring to you because you know all this information. Imagine you were one of my fans. What would you pay to get this information?"

"Just about anything," Mom said.

"I'm going to go look at the damage that was done by the fire. Anybody coming with me?" Mom and Rebecca both got up.

When I got to work this morning, everybody ran over and started asking questions: "Is it true that your parents beat you when you were a kid?"

"Are you really going out with Alice Carlin?"

"Is it true that you know how to speak Indian names?"

"Everybody, shut up!" When everybody was quiet I asked, "Will one person tell me what this is about?" Mark brought forward a magazine, and when I looked down it was an article on Alice.

We all started riding to the pasture when I saw somebody running behind the barn. I broke into a dead run, with Mom and Rebecca following. We pinned him in the corner of the barn. "What is your name?" I asked him. He didn't answer. "Are you the one who's been setting fires around here?" He shook his head. "Mom, will you go get Tyler?"

"Sure." About two minutes later, Mom came back with Tyler.

"What's wrong, Alice?"

"This guy is trespassing and won't talk. Will you please take care of him?"

"Yes, ma'am." Tyler grabbed the guy and led him to the truck. When they were gone, we headed back to our original destination.

When we got there we hopped off our horses and tied them to a tree. We walked out to the fence line. "What is that?" Rebecca asked. Mom and I ran over to her. She pointed to something in the woods.

"Is that a gas can?" Mom asked. Nobody answered her. I pulled my phone from my pocket and snapped a picture. I ran back to Sarge and made him run for all he was worth back home.

When we hit gravel I flew into the jeep. I went speeding down the road. When I pulled into the firefighter parking lot, I crawled out of the jeep and Naomi came running up to me.

"What's wrong? If you're here just to see Keith, then I suggest you come back later. He's kind of surrounded by his men and a few others." I told her the story, and she helped me find Keith. We hung back a couple of minutes when we found Keith to see what was going on.

Somebody handed Keith a magazine, but Keith took one look at it and handed it back. From behind me somebody asked, "Can I help you?" Naomi and I turned around at the same time.

"Can Keith have the day off?" Naomi asked.

He took one look at me and said, "Yes." My attention turned back to Keith. He was speaking.

"I don't know what's in those magazines or what they are about, and I don't intend to read them."

"Why?" somebody asked.

I decided I would get Keith out of this mess for right now. "Because his girlfriend hasn't told him what it's about." The crowd parted and gasped. Keith walked over to me. "Let's go."

"I have to work."

"No, you don't, and neither do you, Naomi. Go with Alice Carlin. See you tomorrow," somebody said from behind me again. It was the chief.

"Thank you," I said. I grabbed both their hands and dragged them to my jeep.

When we were on the road Keith asked, "Will you please tell me what's going on?" Naomi filled him in. Keith looked at me.

"Keith, I'm going to say it." He shook his head. "I think somebody's trying to hurt me."

"Dang it, Alice. Why couldn't you tell Naomi that? Now I have to investigate."

"Good. By the way, our date is tonight."

"Should I be scared?"

"No, this is not mean. I think it's time you learn about the accident."

"Why now?"

"Because you are going to have to tell the boys something tomorrow, and it's just going to be worse."

"Yeah, couldn't you have waited until I stepped outside to take me with you?"

"Sorry, that was my fault. I dragged her in there and I'm glad I did. You would have been in there until ten," Naomi said from the back.

"By the way, you should take James to the bar. I'll call and tell him to meet me there at six."

"Will that work?"

"I'll have my parents pick the girls up at five. He'll think Alice broke up with me and I need moral support in the beer and in him." We pulled up to the barn, and Sarge came to greet us. Then Mom and Rebecca came running. "Is Tyler back?" I asked Rebecca.

"Where did Tyler go?" Keith asked.

"Alice caught somebody sneaking around the barn, and he wouldn't talk, so Tyler took him in. No, he's not back yet. I take that back. Here he comes."

"Sorry, Alice, they couldn't get him to talk, so the only thing they could do was charge him with trespassing," he said when he came over.

"That's okay. I'm going to call and have them waive that charge."

"Why would you do that?" Keith asked.

"Because I have enough enemies and don't need to make more."

"She has a good point," Naomi said. We all got out and saddled horses. When everyone jumped up, Naomi started backing away. I still had Sarge to saddle, but that would take a matter of seconds.

"Naomi, have you ever ridden a horse?" Keith asked.

"No."

"I bet I can saddle this horse in less than two minutes," I said.

"I bet you can't." Nobody said anything. I had a feeling that this would happen, so I already had the stopwatch and saved saddling Sarge until the last.

"How much do you want to bet?"

"If you can't you have to kiss Keith." I looked at Keith.

"Fine, but if I do you have to jump up behind somebody other than Keith or me."

"Deal." We shook hands and I handed her the stopwatch.

"Start." After a little over a minute I yelled, "Stop!" She sat there and stared at the stopwatch.

"One minute, thirty seconds."

"Looks like you're up behind mom or Rebecca."

"Your mom."

Keith, Rebecca, and I jumped on and ran.

Chapter 16

We were all racing down the pasture when Sarge slammed to a complete stop. "Keith, look," she said. Out to the south it looked like another fire. I looked over at Rebecca, and she already had her phone out, probably calling the fire department. "Keith, how much vacation do you have?"

"Four months, why?"

"Are the girls out of school?"

"Yes."

"I'd like to take you to my place in Texas. I'm moving a bunch of horses there."

"Why do you want to take us to Texas?"

"Look at where that fire is." I looked again.

"It looks like it's right over where my house is."

"Keith, whoever is after me is now after you."

"Why?"

"The magazine from yesterday said that you might be my boyfriend."

"So?"

"So if they want to hurt me, the worst thing they could do would be to hurt you and the girls."

"Fine. Take me to my car, and I'll pack bags and get the girls from Mom's."

"Tyler will take you to your car. I have to pack." We rode back hard again. "Tyler, will you take Keith back to his car?"

"Sure." When they were gone, I went to go find Mom and Naomi. I'm sure Rebecca went to go pack her things already. She knows that she doesn't have a choice in whether or not she comes. Naomi and Mom were in the barn.

"Mom, we're going to Texas. We're bringing Keith, Rebecca, the girls, horses, and hopefully Naomi. We're going to need the big plane."

"Why?"

"Somebody's house is on fire by Keith's house, or it is Keith's house. Naomi, will you come with us?"

"Sure I haven't taken a vacation in four years, so I should get it off without a hitch. How long do you think we will be there?"

"I honestly don't know. I have to go pack. Mom, will you bring Naomi into town? I have to make a few arrangements, and I'll call your boss. I am already calling for Keith since your boss seems to like me."

"Thank you. What time are we leaving?"

"As soon as possible. I have my own plane, so it won't take that long to get here. Sorry about your date with James. You can invite him if you want."

"Thanks, I will." Mom and Naomi drove to the fire department. I walked out to the pasture and decided all the horses from the barn and some of the horses from the west pasture were coming.

I went inside and called the plane, Naomi and Keith's work, and started telling the guards. I decided to keep half of my guards here.

Once everybody was told what was going on, I started packing my bags. When my suitcases were packed, I started bringing them to the truck when the phone rang. "Hello?"

"Alice, it's Keith. I just got a call from James, and he said that they were going to Texas."

"Yeah, I know. I invited them to come."

"Can I bring Ayasha with us, then?"

"Of course you can. Why didn't James ask me?"

"First of all, he doesn't have your number, and second, he doesn't have her anymore."

"You brought her home?"

"Yeah. Speaking of bringing her home, James got a new dog. Can she come too?"

"She can too. Make sure they have a leash."

"Why's that?"

"Because there are a lot of people and I'm bringing horses. We have to take the plane with the horse hangar underneath."

"Got to go. The girls are calling me."

"Okay, bye." We both hung up. "After you're done packing, will you help me with the horses?" I asked Mom when she walked over to me.

"Yeah. It won't take that long to pack. Where are we throwing the luggage?"

"In the truck."

"How many horses are we bringing?"

"Only fifty. That's all the plane can hold with all the luggage and the dogs."

"Which fifty, and what's that about dogs?"

"I figure with all the people, I'll take the ones from the barn and the most experienced with flying. I will put Midnight up front. Keith and James are bringing their dogs."

"Okay, I'll go pack and come out." She went into the house and started packing. I went to the barn and grabbed three saddles and bridles. Mom and Rebecca would help me get the horses to the plane. I grabbed all the halters and lead ropes I would need.

When I got in the pasture, all the horses came running up to me. I started putting halters on. After five minutes Mom came to help. "I told Rebecca to hurry up and pack. She said she would come and help when she was done packing."

"Okay, thank you. You don't mind me taking people to Texas do you?"

"No, absolutely not. I am thrilled that you want to take them to Texas. Why would I care? It's your home."

"It's your home too."

"No, you and Michael bought it and kindly let me stay there."

"It's your home, and that's that. I don't know what I would have done without you."

"I don't know what I would have done without you. After your dad died I would have fallen apart if you hadn't needed me. In a way, you were stronger than me."

"You were stronger than me. I never once saw you cry when Daddy died, but when Michael died I blubbered like a baby."

"Honey, I cried a lot when your daddy died. You cried more, yes, but you had twice as many losses in one shot. If I would have lost you and your dad, I would still be crying to this day."

"I was going to tell Keith how Michael was killed tonight, but I'm not going to anymore."

"Why not? He has a right to know."

"I'm not going to tell him tonight because I don't want to tell everybody, especially the girls."

"That makes sense." We had all the horses' halters on.

"I'm going to leave some of the guards here. Make it look like we're still here."

"That's smart. Make sure that you leave Mandy here to cook their meals. I'll cook all our meals."

"Are you sure? That's a lot of meals to prepare."

"Honey, I prepare that many meals when you have Mandy here. Besides, it's bring-your-own-food month."

"That's right. You lucked out."

"I know." Rebecca came walking around the corner.

"Whoa, you got those halters on fast."

"We weren't even concentrating," I said.

"What were you doing?"

"We were just talking."

"Let's get them to the plane. While you were talking you must have missed the plane fly overhead." I was glad I saddled the horses earlier. I hated being late for the plane.

"Is Keith coming soon? There's a storm coming."

"That's convenient." I pulled my phone out of my pocket and called Keith.

"Hello?"

"Hey, Keith, it's Alice. Will you call everybody and see if they're almost ready? You can give them my number, but make sure you tell them not to give it to anybody else. I'll read them the rules when they get here, even though they really don't apply to anybody anymore."

"I'll give it to them and read them the rules."

"Thanks, Keith."

"I'll call you when we're leaving town."

"Thanks, bye."

"Bye." As soon as I got off the phone with Alice, I called Naomi on the way to get the girls. "Hello?"

"Hey, Naomi. It's Keith."

"Hey, Keith. What's up?"

"Do you have Alice's number?"

"No."

"Would you like it?"

"Sure." I gave her Alice's phone number and the rules. "Thanks, Keith. See you soon."

"Make sure you call her before you leave town."

"I will. Thanks again." After we said our good-byes, we hung up. I just pulled up to Mom's house and decided to call James when we were on the road again.

When I got to Mom's and grabbed the girls, they started throwing a fit. "Girls, dry it up. We're going to Texas with Alice." That did it. They stopped throwing a fit immediately.

"We're going to Alice's house?"

"Yeah. How did you know about Alice's house in Texas?"

"We heard you talking about it," Caroline said.

"Bye, Mom and Dad."

"When will you be back?"

"I don't know. Girls, your bags are packed. Are you ready to go?" My cell phone rang. It was James. "Hello?"

"Hey, Keith. Naomi is coming to pick me up and take me to Texas. She said we are going to stay in a mansion."

"I know. I'm going too, considering it's my girlfriend's mansion."

"It's Alice's?"

"Yeah, and how much do you love me?"

"Right now, I don't know. Why?"

"You better start, because would you like her number?"

"Yes!"

"Do you remember the rules?"

"Yes!" Just because he was excited, I read him the rules again and then gave him her number. "Thanks. Got to go. Naomi just arrived."

"Bye, James."

"Bye, Keith." We hung up, and I got the girls into the car. When we hit the outskirts of town, I called Alice.

"Hello?"

"Hey, Alice. It's Keith. We're about five miles away. Did Naomi call you?"

"Yes, they are about four miles away. Have you talked to James?"

"Yeah, he's in with Naomi."

"Do you think they will go out to eat with us tonight? Mom wants the girls, and you and I are kicked out until eight.'"

"What time will we get there?"

"About five, five thirty."

"Do we get to unpack before we have to leave?"

"The way Mom put it was that we get to put our luggage in our rooms and then we had to leave. When we get back I'm supposed to give you a tour of the house."

"See you when we get there."

"Okay, bye."

"Girls, did you have fun at James's house?"

"Yeah, but he didn't seem too happy that you left us there," Caroline said.

"I'm sure he loved having you there."

"We're here!" Jane cried excitedly. Before the car came to a rolling stop, the girls were in Alice's arms, giving each other hugs.

"Put the luggage in back of the white truck!" she yelled to me. When all the luggage was in the truck, I walked over to them. "Are you ready?"

"Yeah, all the luggage is in the truck."

"Are we going to your mansion in Texas?" Caroline asked, not trusting her daddy to have told her the truth.

"Yes, are you okay with that?"

"Yeah!"

"Well, the faster you get in that truck, the faster we can be on our way." The girls ran and jumped into the truck. She turned to me. "Can you drive the truck?"

"Sure, but I don't know where I'm going."

"That's okay. You'll just follow Mom, Rebecca, and me on the horses. We're still rounding up the horses so we can get them on the plane." I nodded my head, and we went our different ways. She jumped up on Sarge, and I got in the driver's seat of the truck.

Her mom and Rebecca came to join her. It looked like she was telling them what she wanted done.

When she was done they took off and started herding the horses into a pasture. When one started getting out of order, Alice was on him. She'd grab a lead rope, hook it on its halter, and bring it back. If it would stop to eat, she would get behind it and bump into it until it went.

The whole point of Casey and Rebecca being there was to show the perimeters and where to go. All of a sudden, two horses that I recognized broke out of the perimeter and shot across the field. It was Dakota and Leo. Alice broke out in a run behind them. Rebecca moved to the front and Casey moved to the back of the line. We were all watching Alice in the truck.

She pulled something off her saddle and started whipping it over her head. Sarge knew exactly what she was doing because he kicked it into another gear. They were in a full-out run when she threw the loop that she had been whirling above her head. It caught around Dakota's neck, and she turned around and started riding back. She pulled Dakota, and Leo followed.

She went back to all the other horses and pulled the loop off Dakota's neck. She shook her head and started laughing. It sounded like she said, "It happens every time." Then she looked back and pointed back toward the front of the horses. When I peered forward, I saw what she was pointing at. The plane was sitting there.

Casey and Rebecca hopped off and started hooking lead ropes to horses. Alice rode over and said, "Bring the luggage over there and they will load it." She went back to the horses and yelled something. They all started to load into the plane.

I drove the truck to where she told me to go, and true to her words, they started unloading the truck. Somebody came out and ushered us to the cab in the plane. We all just went and sat down. "There are certain spots you have to sit in," the lady said. Pointing to the first two seats, she said, "Keith, you are here with Alice." When I gave her a mystified look, she said, "I got orders from Casey." Then she pointed to the second row of seats. "James and Naomi, you sit here." She pointed to the row behind them and said, "Girls, you sit here. Rebecca and Casey will be sitting in back, and she said they would be watching you, so don't do anything dumb." We all started laughing. She left, and Alice, Casey, and Rebecca came walking in.

"What's so funny?" Casey asked.

"We'll be watching you," I said.

"We will." Over the intercom the pilot said, "Please buckle your seatbelts." We all started to buckle our seat belts.

"A little warning, I'll fall asleep," Alice said. It wasn't two minutes and she was asleep.

I watched the scenery go by while Alice slept. It was pretty. Then I saw a huge barn with a white picket fence around it. There were pastures for as far as I could see. The intercom came on and asked us to fasten our seatbelts again. Alice woke up. "Welcome home, Mom!" she yelled.

"Welcome home, honey."

"Welcome back, Rebecca."

Welcome home, Alice."

"Welcome to my home!" she yelled to everybody else. Nobody answered her. We were all staring out the window with our jaws hanging open.

Chapter 17

When the plane came to a stop, Alice was the first out the door. Then it was Casey, Rebecca, the girls, me, Naomi, and finally James. "James, look at me!" Alice yelled. When he looked she snapped a picture of him. She handed the camera to Casey and ran to James's side. She kissed his cheek, and Casey snapped the picture. "I'll get you the pictures when we get in the house."

"What was that for?" James asked.

I was surprised at how jealous I was that she kissed James and not me.

"When I first met you, you wanted my picture and phone number. Now you can have it. Don't look so cheated, Keith. You'll get one too, just not right now. In fact, you will have a lot of pictures taken." James started laughing. "James, you get the picture when you ask Naomi on a double date with us tonight."

"The first day here and you are going on a date?" he said in disbelief.

"We are kicked out until eight."

"Sure, I'll ask," Casey snuck up behind him and said.

"You better, 'cause you and Naomi are kicked out until eight too. Alice will give you a tour when you get back."

"That's if I'm not passed out. I'm hitting the bar, whether you like it or not."

"Fine, but I'm calling the bar and telling them you can only have one beer. You are not going to have a hangover tomorrow. Keith, she can have one beer and a couple glasses of wine. Alice, where do you want the horses?"

"Put them in the west corral. I'll put them where they're supposed to be in the morning."

"Put your stuff inside the door and leave. Even better, leave now, because the guards just took your luggage inside." We turned and left. James went to go ask Naomi on a date and tell her the news. When Alice and I got in the limo, I asked her, "Where are we going first?"

"We're going to dinner and then to the bar. Every time I fly I always go to the bar the same night. After Michael's funeral I flew home to Evansville and got really drunk. That's why Mom said only one beer. I can withstand a lot of wine. I haven't flown much since then because my job doesn't demand it."

"That makes sense. If I hadn't had the girls, I would have gone to the bar and gotten drunk too." James and Naomi climbed in, and we headed for dinner. Alice and I sat on one side and Naomi and James on the other.

We all watched out the window as we drove to the restaurant. "If you don't want your picture taken, I suggest you do not hang out with me. Keith, if you're not in one picture, my mom might have your hide," Alice said.

"Well, I certainly don't want your mom to have my hide, and I certainly don't plan on leaving your side."

"I don't mind pictures," Naomi said.

"This is a double date, and I don't plan on ruining it," James said.

"Thanks, but if it gets to be too much for you, feel free to leave. I'm going to have to deal with my fans and paparazzi, so it might be a half an hour before we get in to eat." We pulled up to the restaurant, and Alice looked at the driver then looked at Naomi. "Come with me, Naomi." They walked to the back of the limo, where there were no windows. A curtain fell, and after a couple of minutes, they came out. They were both in summer dresses. Alice looked at the driver again and nodded her head. A mirror and makeup fell down. She fixed her makeup and then nodded again. A purse dropped down. She nodded, and a bunch of stuff fell into the purse. Then she looked at James and me. "Boys, go in back and change."

We walked to where she and Naomi had gone and found dressing rooms with our names on them. When we were done, we went back to the front. When we got there Alice nodded her head and everything folded back up. "Is everybody ready?"

"Yeah," everybody said at the same time. We all started getting out of the car. When Alice and I got out, the cameras started flashing. She held my hand and gave me a reassuring squeeze. We started walking to the restaurant when we heard two girls squeal from the crowd. They ran up to the front of the crowd and asked for autographs. I now understood why she dumped all that stuff in her purse. She did it so she doesn't have to sign everything as she goes. She can just hand out her picture with her autograph.

After a half hour, we finally made it to our seats. "We get to eat for free," Alice said.

"Why?" James asked.

"Because you are with me and I draw a lot of attention. If I'm in here and they come in, they have to eat."

"So they make a big profit, and to keep you coming they give you free food?" I said.

"Pretty much." She waved over a waiter and looked at him very seriously and said, "Is my usual waiter in?"

"Yes, ma'am. I'll get him right away. Can I get your order for drinks?"

"Sure." We all gave him an order for our beverages and he left. Another waiter came back with our drinks. He nodded to Alice, and she nodded back. He took our order and left.

When we looked over, there was a man with a camera trying to get pictures. Alice and I looked away. She waved over the waiter again. "That man with the camera? Kindly remind him he can't take pictures when we're eating. Since we are not eating, will you please get us some salads?" He grabbed her pop and went to the back.

"Why did he take your pop?" I asked her.

"He has to make it look like I called him over for a reason. He'll take my pop like he's going to go refill it, and very conveniently our salads will be done, so he will bring them out with my pop."

"That's smart."

"I know. I taught him a few tricks. He's my waiter every time I come in here. He's the owner's son, so people listen to him."

"What if you come in and he's not on duty?"

"I get taken back to a private room, and he comes in. When he gets in he personally escorts me to my seat. My seat is the same one every time. This is my table because everybody in this restaurant can see me but the people outside cannot."

"That's really smart too. If they come in they have to eat something."

"Hey, look, my favorite cowboy is here," she said. Our food came with Alice's pop. The cowboy started walking over, but the waiter went to go stop him. Alice quickly caught his arm. "Brady is with us." The waiter nodded and went to go talk to the guy with the camera. The guy argued, but when the waiter told him he would have to kick him out, he shut his mouth and obeyed.

When the cowboy got close Alice stood up and gave him a hug. She told him to take a seat right by Naomi. "Keith, Naomi, James, this is Brady. Brady was like my brother from another mother. Brady grew up in Brandon, but he was always at my house riding my horses. I introduced him to my best friend in school, and they wound up getting married."

"Nice to see you, Alice. I heard you were back in town."

"Yeah, how is your Olivia doing?"

"Great. She is expecting."

"Really? When is she due?"

"Next month. Speaking of my wife, I better get what she wants, or she will be hurling salt and pepper shakers at me when I get home. You should stop by and see her sometime. I know she would love to see you."

"I will. Tell her I said hi." He left, and the waiter brought our main dish. We all dug in.

We broke up the conversation into two groups. Alice started talking. "I admire that you want to hear my story from me. I think it's time that I tell you." She paused, and I didn't push. "I was coming home from town when I spotted this horse rearing and backing up from this man. She was trying to get away from the whip. I pulled over and was going to call Michael. He would know what to do. But before I pressed send, a woman ran out and started screaming at him. He didn't respond to that well and hit her with the whip. I could see that he smacked her hard, 'cause she was bleeding. She ran to her car and sped away.

"I threw my phone in the seat next to me and quickly drove home. When I flew through the door, Michael was trying to get up. He was as white as a ghost, but that didn't register as something was wrong. I was too upset. I told him the story, and he made sure the girl was safe and then said to leave the horse. I would have none of that and told him that if he didn't come with me, I was going to go by myself. He knew that I was serious and didn't want me to go alone.

"We got there and waited for the guy to finish his beers and pass out. We went back to the stables and found her lying there all cut up and bloody. My stomach couldn't handle it, so I had to leave. I could hear the palomino freaking out at Michael and Michael soothing her with words.

Finally all the noise quit and I walked in. Michael was leading her to the trailer. When she was loaded, he went and checked the man's heartbeat. There was none. He had drunk himself into his grave.

"We got back into the truck and started heading home. It finally occurred to me that Michael was as white as a ghost, so I made him pull over to the side of the road. I told him to let me drive, but he said that I shouldn't be driving since I only had one month until my due date. I told him that if he didn't let me drive that I would walk home. He thought that it would be better if he let me drive because he knew that I would walk the ten miles home. We were five miles from home when I saw the cow in the road. I went to swerve around it, but the baby kicked really hard and I pulled the wheel too hard. We shot sideways. I couldn't get the wheel turned. I had the cruise on because my feet started to hurt. I couldn't get it off, and so I tried to swerve to miss the tree, but I didn't have enough strength.

"We hit the tree, and all I remember is everything turning black. I woke up in the ambulance. My stomach hurt so bad. It took the paramedics a while to convince me to let them look at the baby.

"When we got to the hospital they pronounced the baby dead, and same with my husband. When they finally said that I could leave the hospital, I waited until the dead of night. When the paparazzi tried to find me, I left and hid; and when they found me I would run and hide again. That's why my story is so big that everybody is willing to do anything to get to me. Do you hate me now that you know my story?"

"No. You tried all you could." When Alice got halfway

through her steak, she asked to be excused. Naomi asked to be excused too. They went to the ladies' room.

James looked at me funny when they were out of sight. "What?"

"You got really jealous when she hugged that cowboy didn't you?"

"Was it that obvious?"

"Yes." We sat in silence for a little while, but James finally broke down and asked the obvious question. "What do you think they're talking about?"

"I don't know. I think Alice is almost done with her steak, so maybe they're fixing their makeup again. You know as well as I do that it's going to be a zoo when we step outside those doors. There's going to be cameras flashing like crazy." The waiter came out and asked James and Keith to go to the men's room. Some lady had dropped something off and said that they had to wear it all.

Naomi and I got up to use the restrooms at the same time. She must have got my look I shot in her direction that said, "Follow me."

When Naomi got into the bathroom, she spun around to face me and asked, "What's wrong?"

"I think Keith and I are going to sneak out the back doors."

"Why?"

"I don't know how much more paparazzi I can take tonight, and we still have to hit the bar," a girl that worked there came out of a stall and said. "Sorry to ruin your plans, but your mom has a different idea of what you should do tonight. Alice, go to the end stall, and, Naomi, go to the first stall, and put on what's in there."

"What if we don't want to?" I asked.

"Then your mom will have your hide and you will be locked out until one." Naomi went to her stall, and I walked to mine.

In my stall was the red dress that I wore the first day the paparazzi found me. I quickly threw on the dress.

When I stepped out of the stall I got makeup thrust at me. "Put it on," She commanded.

I got most of my makeup on by the time Naomi stepped out of her stall. She got makeup thrown at her too. "How did you get dressed so fast?"

"Years of practice." I quickly finished my makeup. "Can I do your makeup? Before I became a model I was going to become a beautician."

"Sure. I feel retarded."

"Don't you ever wear dresses?"

"Yeah, but not like this. I'm not going to a ball." Just as she said that I got a text message. It said, "Keith and James are in the men's room getting ready for the ball. Have fun."

"I'm pretty sure we are going to a ball." I handed her the phone and started doing her makeup. When we both had our makeup done, a hair designer came in and did our hair up like we were in a wedding.

When we had our makeover done top to bottom, we were ushered out. Keith and James were standing by the table in tuxes and reading a text message off Keith's phone. "I think Keith just got the same text message that we did," I told

Naomi. We continued walking over to them. Keith looked up at me with a questioning look. "I have no clue what she's up to, but we are hitting the bar first. Keith, you better let me have more than one beer, because I'm going to need it." Nobody said anything more. We just ran to the limo.

When we entered the limo I said, "We don't have to go." Right after I said that, I got another text message. Everybody leaned over to read it. "If you don't go to the ball, the doors will be locked until three."

"What is she doing? Watching us?" James asked. That was exactly what she was doing. I looked around for anything that might carry a microphone in it, or even a camera. Then it hit me. Naomi's purse.

"Naomi, let me see your purse." She looked confused but handed over her purse. I looked in the big pocket, and sure enough there was a little microphone in the pocket. "Got it. You lose," I said into the microphone before I threw it out the window.

I gave Naomi her purse back and another text came in. It said, "You found that one, but you have not found all." I looked for more things that might carry a microphone. Keith and James had a flower sticking out of their pockets. I quickly grabbed Keith's and threw it out the window. Naomi, catching on to the game, grabbed James's and threw it out the window. I picked up my right foot and found a microphone underneath. Naomi picked up her right foot and found nothing, so she picked up her left foot and there was one there. Another text came in. "Very good, but I sill have people that will vouch if you are there or not."

"I think we got all of them based on that message," I said.

Chapter 18

We pulled up to where the ball was taking place. It was in my barn. Rebecca and mom had been up to no good again. "You didn't know you were throwing a ball?" Naomi asked.

"This morning when we were getting horses ready to load, we were fighting over who's house this is. Mom said it was mine, but I said it was both of ours. She took that a little too seriously."

"So because it's both of your property, she decided to throw a ball without telling you?" Naomi asked.

"She and Rebecca." We all got out of the car and started going to the barn.

We walked through all the stalls and greeted all the horses I hadn't seen in a long time. We walked upstairs, and I was surprised at how many people were there. When we walked in the room, everybody yelled, "Happy Birthday!" Keith looked at me like I was the stupidest person alive for not remembering my own birthday. I turned around to start heading to the house, but Keith grabbed my arm and Naomi and James blocked my exit.

The girls ran over and gave me a hug. They each grabbed a hand and pulled me over to where Mom and Rebecca were standing. "You two really suck," I said.

"You forgot it was your birthday again. Do you know how old you are today?" Rebecca asked.

"I'm twenty-nine for another hour and ten minutes."

Mom said, "Sorry, honey, it's your thirtieth birthday. Your party was going to be at the ranch, but you decided to come here. I didn't pack my suitcase. I called Rebecca and Noah, and together we called everybody. Your plane would have been a little late if you wouldn't have decided to bring the horse, because it was out getting people here."

"I hate you both for this." I went to find Keith, Naomi, and James. Mom was following until Noah stopped her.

He turned to me and shook his head. "I'm sorry, Alice. I tried to talk them out of it."

"Why?"

"I know you were planning to do a thirtieth birthday party for Michael. It was supposed to be in the barn here. You had a guest list that went down the wall."

"I forgot about that."

"All the plans are still hanging in the room. I remember how you and Michael used to fight because you never let him in the room."

"I forgot about that. I haven't been in the house yet. Mom said that we couldn't enter until eight." I wouldn't tell Noah the real reason that I hadn't been in the mansion yet. I hadn't been in the house because it hurt too much. *Michael, why did you have to go?* I thought. *Maybe if Keith's with me it won't hurt so much.*

"Your mom will let you enter the house now. She just said that so you would get away from the house."

"I would be in my house if I weren't talking to you. Now that that point is made, will you excuse me?" I started walking away. When I looked back I could tell Noah knew how much trouble I was having being here. *I have to escape. I can't be in here without my husband's arms around me.* That voice that I always heard when I wanted Michael came in my head: "Alice, Michael's not coming back because you killed him and your baby." I ran out of the barn and headed to the house as fast as I could in heels.

Alice had gone with the girls to go see Casey and Rebecca. James and Naomi went to go dance. After five minutes I went looking for Casey. I got halfway there when Noah stopped me. Noah asked, "Where is Alice?"

"With Casey and Rebecca."

"No, I talked to her after that. I thought she went to go find you after she was done talking to me. She was going to show people the house."

"I haven't seen her."

"We better find her because you have a dance."

"We have a dance?"

"You and her, Rebecca and I, and Naomi and James."

"You and Rebecca?" I raised one eyebrow.

He laughed and said, "Yeah she is a great dancer. We always have at least one dance."

"How good is Alice?"

"Really good if you can lead in slow dancing."

"What are we dancing to?"

"Can you slow dance?"

"Yeah."

"Then you'll be fine. Let's go find Alice."

"I don't know my way around."

"That's fine. I do."

"Then why do you need me?"

"Because you're going to be the only one to get her out of hiding."

"Fine. Let's go." He led me into the mansion and to a door. "What's this room?"

"This is the room that anything Alice didn't want Michael to see went into. When I talked to her I brought up a memory, and she didn't react to it very well."

"You are stupid. I've already learned not to bring up the subject. When she remembers, she tells you." I knocked on the door. "Alice, will you let me in?"

"Only if Noah disappears." I looked at Noah. "What time is the dance?"

"In ten minutes."

"Make them stall for about twenty." He nodded and disappeared. "Alice, honey, Noah is gone. Will you let me in?" She opened it a crack and then quickly closed it. I heard the door lock click.

"I don't want to talk to you."

"Who do you want to talk to?"

"Naomi." I turned to go get Naomi.

When I got back to the barn, Casey and Rebecca came running. I walked past them and onto the dance floor. I came up behind James and tapped on his shoulder. He turned to look at me, and I quickly took his place. I twirled Naomi out of the dance floor and toward the exit.

Once we were safely outside she said, "James is going to kill you later."

"I hope you like dancing with him, because you have to dance with him in front of everybody."

"Why did you take me away from him?"

"Because I have to dance with Alice, and she is hiding. She won't talk to anybody but you." I pulled her to the room Alice was in and started going back to the barn.

On the other side of the door I could hear two people walking. I heard them stop and heard one walking away. It must be Keith and Naomi. There was a knock on the door and then, "Alice, open up please." I switched the lock again and opened the door.

She walked in and closed the door behind her. She looked at everything, and I could tell she was pondering what everything was. "What is all this?" she finally asked.

"This is the room I wouldn't let Michael into because I was planning his thirtieth birthday party. What they did for mine was exactly what I was going to do for his. There is only one thing missing. Our dance."

"I've got news for you: there is a dance for you. It's not with Michael, but it is with Keith."

"Crap."

"I thought you didn't like bad language?"

"I don't, but I've had a couple of glasses of wine. Is Keith good at dancing?"

"He's better than James. Come on; let's go. If we don't hurry up we are going to have an abundance of people banging down that door, and I wouldn't put it past Keith and Noah to break down the door."

"After this party we are going to go to my room and get a body massage."

"Okay, but where is my room going to be?"

"Right across from mine. I'll show you." I was showing her the room when Noah and James came running down the hallway. "What is going on? Noah, this better be important. You know the no-running rule."

"One of the horses is really upset," Noah said. *Why would one of the horses be upset? The only reason would be if one of the mares was in heat.*

"Are there any studs out there?"

"Yes. Dakota and Ghost."

"Let's go. Midnight should be in heat. Did Mom separate any of the horses?"

"No." I flipped off my heels and bee-lined it to the pasture. When I got to the barn, I threw on my boots and grabbed a halter. When I was in the pasture I ran to Midnight and put her halter on her. We raced into stall number three. She still limped from her surgery.

Noah, Naomi, and James were walking into the barn as I was running up the stairs. Keith met me at the top of the stairs. "Are you okay?" he asked, sounding really concerned.

"Yeah. How long do we have until we dance?"

"About two minutes."

"Good, let's go yell at my mom." We were walking toward Mom and Rebecca when Rebecca came flying past us toward Noah. I looked up at Mom, and she nodded. Everybody started pushing us toward the middle of the dance floor. I helped them out and pulled Keith to the middle of the dance floor.

When we were all out in the middle of the dance floor, they started the music. I laughed. They were playing one of my favorite songs to slow dance to. It was "Love as True as Mine."

"When the song ended, we went different ways. I went to the sidelines, and Keith went to go find the girls. James followed Keith, and Noah went to go find Mom. Their partners came over to me. Rebecca asked, "Are you ready?"

"Ready for what?" Naomi asked.

"Do you know the dance moves to 'We're Young and Beautiful'?"

"No, Rebecca. Absolutely not!" I yelled.

"Yes, we are. Don't make me go get Noah over here."

"I love that song," Naomi stated.

"Good. You can dance with the rest of the group," Rebecca told her. They each grabbed a hand and pulled. When they had me in the middle of the circle in the dance floor, the music started again. We danced for two hours because Rebecca wouldn't let me go. Finally I made a speech and went to bed.

Chapter 19

Two weeks later...

We were all packing to get ready to leave when the pilot came running into the house. He said, "Keith, your mom's in the hospital. I got a call that I'm supposed to take you and the girls to the hospital immediately."

"What's wrong?" Alice asked from the doorway.

"My mom's in the hospital."

"I'm sorry, Keith. Let's go. I'll get the girls." Alice disappeared and then the pilot. About two minutes later, Alice was holding Jane and Caroline was in my arms.

"Daddy, is Grandma going to be okay?" Caroline asked. Jane pulled away from Alice long enough to hear my answer.

"I hope so."

"Keith, we should go so you can find out what's going on," Alice said. We each grabbed a girl and ran to the jet. We got our seatbelts on, and the jet started going up. An hour later we landed at the hospital parking lot. Dad came out to meet us, and the girls went running into his arms. When he looked up it looked like he had been crying for hours. "Dad, what happened?"

"She was reading a magazine when she said, 'No, that can't be.' When I asked her what couldn't be, she passed out and fell to the floor. I tried to catch her, but I was too slow."

"Dad, I'm sure it's not your fault."

"Keith, what magazine was she reading?" Alice asked. Before I could answer, Dad did.

"The one you are." Alice turned the magazine around.

"Is this the article she was reading?" Dad nodded, and she turned to face me. "Your mom has taken a liking to reading articles about us." I groaned and she continued, "This one says we are engaged." Dad was shaking his head with the "I can't believe you didn't tell us" look on his face. The girls looked so miserable. If it was the idea of Alice and me getting married or about their grandma, I don't know.

"Somebody has to call and set them straight," I said a little too forcefully. A nurse came running over to us.

"She is yelling for her son, his girlfriend, and her grand-children. It is not good for her to get worked up after her heart attack."

"Heart attack?" Alice asked.

"She is suffering from a heart attack. At the moment she has no power over her legs." We rushed in after hearing that.

After we got in the room, Alice set her straight about being engaged. They talked for half an hour before Alice stepped back. After an hour the nurse came in and said she needed to rest.

When we were in the hallway, Alice stopped me and flagged everybody else forward. "I'm canceling our date tonight," she stated.

"Why?"

"Because you need to be here with your family. I'm going to go home to Texas."

"Why? Why don't you stay here?"

"I'm not family and—"

I interrupted her, "You are family in my book. Please stay. I know the girls would love it if you stayed."

"Fine. I'll stay." I didn't even think about what I was doing, but I bent down and covered her mouth with mine. Fireworks were going off. When we broke off, she put her hands to her lips.

"Not the perfect place for the first kiss." Dad came around the corner.

He said, "Hey, you two lovebirds, you want to go get something to eat with us?"

"Sure," Alice said. We followed him out to the car. When we all got seated and going, a phone went off. Alice opened her purse and answered her phone. "Hello?" She listened for a while and then said, "She had a heart attack reading an article about Keith and me." She listened for a while and then said, "Bye, James. I'll call you with an update later." She flipped the phone shut and looked at Jane. Jane hadn't left Alice's side since she found out about Grandma.

After we left the restaurant we went back to the hospital. Keith's dad decided to stay, even though his wife was still asleep. Keith decided that the girls wouldn't be able to sit still very long, so we took them to the park.

The park was completely empty except for one family. Keith told the girls to go play, but Jane stayed at my side and Caroline went to go sit on the swing. We were trying to get Jane to talk, and when I looked up, it looked like Caroline was crying. I handed Jane to Keith and went to go sit by Caroline on the swing.

When I sat on the swing right next to her, she looked up. "Caroline, will you tell me what's wrong?" With tears running down her cheeks she nodded but didn't say anything. I didn't push her. I just waited. She finally started to talk.

"Is she going to be okay?"

"I truly think she will be fine."

"Are you and Daddy boyfriend and girlfriend?"

"Yes. Do you have a boyfriend?"

"No, Daddy said I'm not allowed to date until I'm thirty. As old as you are."

"You know, that's what my daddy said too, but I started dating when I was fourteen."

"Do you think you can tell Daddy that story so he might change his mind?"

"I can try." The huge smile I was working for came.

"Do you love my daddy?"

"Yes, I do." She grew very quiet and her smile disappeared.

"I'm glad you like my daddy, because I like you."

"I like you too. You are one of the sweetest girls I've ever met." Her smile came back. She turned and ran to stand by Keith and Jane. Keith bent down and kissed them and whispered something in their ears. They came racing over to me, and when I gave them a kiss, they asked me if I would go on a date with their daddy. When I shook my head no, Keith yelled, "Why?"

I bent over and whispered in their ear, "Your daddy didn't give me a kiss."

Alice was telling the girls a secret that wouldn't be a secret very long because they came racing back to me. They pulled me down to their height, and Jane whispered, "Alice said no cause you didn't give her a kiss."

"So Alice feels left out and wants a kiss." They both nodded. "Should I give Alice a kiss?" Jane shook her head and Caroline nodded her head. "Why shouldn't I give Alice a kiss, Jane?"

"Kisses are yucky, unless you get them from your daddy."

"Keep thinking that way forever. Why should I, Caroline?"

"Because she loves you and you love her."

"That's not the only reason. I know you too well."

"Fine, that way she can tell you the story of how her daddy said that she couldn't date until she was thirty too."

"I like Jane's idea better. Kisses are yucky."

"No kisses are sweet. We better go. Mom just called and said they are almost here," Alice said from behind. Jane ran over to join Alice in the walk back to the hospital.

Casey, James, Rebecca, and Naomi were standing by the doors to meet us. We were talking when Jane had to go potty, so Alice took her to the bathrooms. They all started yelling questions when we got to the waiting room. "How is she?"

"What happened?"

"Where is your dad?"

"Where is Alice?"

"Mom is doing fine. She had a heart attack reading an article about Alice and me. Dad is in with Mom, and Alice is … where did Alice go, Jane?"

"There she is," Naomi said, pointing toward the door. We all turned to see Noah and Alice shoving cameras out of the doorway.

"The joys of being famous," Casey said. An abundance of nurses and doctors went to help them get the reporters out.

Alice and Noah backed up to join us. Alice came to stand by me, and the girls ran and hugged her legs. A doctor walked over and said, "Sorry about that."

"It's okay. What's the latest on my mother?"

"She is going to be fine. She can go home tomorrow, but she will have to take it easy. If she keeps asking for something, give it to her, especially if it is her grandchildren."

"Okay, thank you."

"You all need to go home. It's not healthy for you to be here around the clock."

"We will. What time will she be released?"

"Noon tomorrow if everything is fine tonight.

"Thanks." He left, and we started filing out of the hospital

Noah, Rebecca, Casey, James, and Naomi all got in the car they came in, and so Alice was with us. Not that I was complaining. The girls jumped in the backseat, and I opened the door for Alice.

Chapter 20

We were on our way to Keith's house when Mom did three blinks with her right blinker and then two with her left. It was the signal for "follow me."

"Keith, go to the ranch."

"Why?"

"Mom must have something to tell us." Keith started to head for the ranch behind Mom when she took a sharp left and Keith followed. She was going way past the speed limit.

"Should I continue following her?"

"Yes, follow her. See where she is going." We followed them to the fire station. Mom pulled into the parking lot and parked. Keith did the same thing, and we got out. When we were standing there waiting for everybody else to join us, everybody in the station came running at us.

They patted Keith on the back and gave me a hug. I looked at Keith, and he shrugged. The girls slowly started getting out of the car. They took one look at Keith and ran over to me.

Naomi was looking over at a guy by the first-responders ambulance when his beeper went off. Even though she wasn't on duty, she ran and jumped in the ambulance. They put on their sirens, and everybody moved out of the way. They shot out of the parking lot and disappeared around the corner.

Keith walked over to James, and they both shrugged at each other. Mom and Rebecca came to stand by me. Mom asked, "Do you know why we brought you here?"

"No."

"To set people straight."

"What! To set people straight about what?"

"About where you and Keith's relationship is at. People from the squad keep calling Naomi and asking her. She sets them straight, but there are a lot of people on this squad." I looked at Rebecca, and she just nodded, seconding what Mom just said.

I turned to Keith and said, "I know what this is all about."

"What?"

"What did your mom just have a heart attack from? Maybe they still haven't given up reading the magazines. We are the hot topic right now." I could tell he figured it out by the way his jaw was set. Most people wouldn't realize the way his jaw was set or be able tell his mood just by looking at him.

He yelled, "We're not engaged!" He mumbled, "Stupid press." Everybody shook their heads and walked away.

I walked over to Keith with the girls hanging on my legs just as the ambulance drove in. The girls transferred over to Keith when Naomi started walking over. She was in full uniform. I asked, "How did you get into your full uniform? You were wearing an everyday outfit when you got in the ambulance."

"I always keep a uniform in the back," she said when she got over to the group of us. James went over and gave her a hug.

"What happened?" he asked.

"Somebody passed out and her son panicked. I used Alice as an example that you could pass out and be fine." Everybody turned to look at me.

Naomi said, "I used Alice as an example because he had pictures of her hanging in his room. They were on every inch of his wall, to be exact."

"What was his name?" Alice asked.

"Cobalt."

"His mother's name didn't happen to be Alyssia, did it?"

"Yes." Alice looked at Casey, and they gave each other devastated looks. "What is it, Alice?"

"She has a problem, and they gave her three years. It has been six, so they figured she would be fine. Cobalt knows his mom has a problem and is supposed to watch over her very carefully. Keith, do you remember how I said I volunteer at the school?" He nodded. "It's because that way Cobalt gets used to me and is not always depending on his mother. I am his godparent." Alice and Casey jumped into a car and went flying out of the parking lot.

We all tried to fit in my car, but we had two too many

people. Naomi grabbed Caroline and they ran to the ambulance. Naomi yelled over her shoulder that she would lead the way. Naomi, her partner, and Caroline jumped in the ambulance and took off with us right on her tail.

When we got there, Naomi and her partner met us at the door while the girls sat in the car. We all said our names, and Casey let us in. She had a little boy in her arms, crying. "Keith, will you please go get my daughter off her?" she asked me, sounding really stressed.

I walked over to where Casey inclined her head and found Alice lying on the still body. "Alice, come here." She looked up, obviously not hearing anybody enter the room. She slowly got up, and when I opened my arms, she ran into them. "Honey, it's going to be okay."

Naomi and her partner walked in with a stretcher and carefully placed the still body on it. They left carrying her with them. Alice watched them leave and then started crying harder. I slowly pulled her into the other room. Noah was holding Rebecca, and Casey was still holding Cobalt. Alice pulled away and grabbed Cobalt from Casey. He snuggled into her and they started down the hallway. We all started to follow, but Alice turned around and told us to stay.

Chapter 21

Two weeks later...

It's been almost a month since Alyssia died, and school is supposed to start in a week. I don't think Cobalt is ready to go back. He still cries for his mommy every night. I do the best to comfort him, knowing his mom is hard to replace.

Keith calls every night to see how we are doing. He normally calls at about the same time every night, so he hears Cobalt crying for his mommy. Tonight he has to work late, so by the time he calls, Cobalt should be asleep.

Cobalt fell asleep early tonight, and Keith wasn't supposed to call until after ten. I decided to go out and ride. I saddled up Sarge, and we started up the cabin trail. We took off in a dead run.

If Keith called, Mom could answer it, and if Cobalt woke up, Mom could tend to him. Knowing they were taken care of, I let all my worry slip off as we ran.

When we made it to the top, I jumped off and Sarge went to graze. I went and sat on the log and started exploring my feelings. I loved the girls like they were my own. I loved Cobalt, and nothing could ever hurt that love. I loved Keith, but I also loved Michael. Would Michael care if I got married again? I knew the answer to that question. He wouldn't want me to be unhappy, but I felt like I was breaking my marriage vows. I loved the child we had together, and nobody or anything could take her place. I finally decided I couldn't make this work without somebody else's help. Somebody greater and more powerful. I folded my hands and bowed my head.

"Dear God, I know it's been a while, but I need your help. I'm so confused. I loved Michael and Haley, but they are gone. Nobody can replace what spots they have in my heart, but I have a lot of love to give.

"I love Keith and the girls. The girls are so sweet, and I think they like me. They have been through so much, Lord. If it is not your will for Keith and me to be together, then don't let it break those little girls' hearts.

"I know Cobalt is starting to cope with his mother's death. Why did you take that little boy's mother away? You probably had someplace better for her to be. Please help Cobalt through this. I know you never give us burdens we cannot handle, but sometimes it seems like it.

"If you could help me work through my emotions and put me on the right path, I would be deeply grateful. Amen."

Sarge came trotting up, and I jumped on. We started on the run back.

When I got back into the house, the phone rang. Mom started to get up but saw me and backed off. I ran to answer it. "Hello?"

"Alice, it's me."

"Hey, how was work today?"

"Good."

"How many times did you have to play twenty questions?"

"Twice. I bet you could never guess who they were."

"It wouldn't happen to be two lovebirds, would it?"

"Yes, but which ones?"

"Naomi and James."

"That's it. How come you sounded out of breath when you answered the phone?"

"Because I ran in from the barn, and then the phone rang so I ran to the phone."

"So I had perfect timing?"

"Yes, you did. How are the girls?"

"Good, I think. Grandma still gets what she wants, so I never get to see my kids."

"Have to go. I hear Cobalt getting up."

"Love you. Bye."

"Love you too." I quickly hung up the phone and went to go see what was wrong with Cobalt. When I got to his room he was tossing around on his bed, having a nightmare. He'd been having them a lot lately.

Chapter 22

One month later...

The girls got home from Grandma and Grandpa's house and ran straight to their room to pack their school bags with what they would need for tomorrow.

When I entered their room, they both looked up at me. "Girls, can we talk?" They both nodded. "How much do you like Alice and Cobalt?"

Caroline started to say, "Cobalt is really nice and smart."

Jane cut her off. "I love Alice like she was my own mommy, and Cobalt is really nice. I wish he were my brother."

Caroline picked up where she left off. "I love Alice. She is really funny and has horses. I want a new mommy, Daddy."

"What would you guys think if I asked Alice to marry me? You would have a new mommy, brother, and grandma." Jane's eyes popped out of her sockets and Caroline didn't move.

After serious thought, Caroline said, "All I want is for you to be happy."

"Me too," Jane said. I grabbed them both and gave them a bear hug.

I dropped by the jewelry store yesterday and picked out an engagement ring on my way home from work. The little red box in my pocket suddenly felt like a million pounds. *When I call Alice tonight, I'll talk to Casey first.*

Two hours later, I called Casey.

"Hello?"

"Hey, Casey, it's Keith. I have a huge favor to ask you."

"What's up?"

"Do you think you could watch the girls and Cobalt tomorrow?"

"Sure. Why? Don't you two normally take them with you?"

"Yes, but this is not a normal date."

"It's about time."

"Whatever, Casey. Is she there?"

"Yes, I'll go get her." The phone went full of static as she set it down. About five minutes later, Alice picked up the phone.

"Sorry about that. Cobalt didn't want me to go."

"Sounds like things are good there."

"Yeah. He finally went to sleep peacefully. I only had to read him six stories."

"Do you want to go out tomorrow night? Just the two of us?"

"Sure. Where are we going?"

"That's for me to know and you to find out, but make sure you wear blue jeans. Don't ask questions. I got to go. Bye."

"Bye."

I quickly hung up the phone so I didn't slip.

The next morning when I showed up for work, I was immediately surrounded by everybody. "What's up now?" They threw a magazine at me. The page they flipped it to had one picture on it and it was of me kissing Alice. "So they did get that picture."

"You kissed her?" the chief yelled from behind. "Come, boy. Come talk to me." Everybody made a path for me. "Get back to work." I followed him into his office. "Keith, how are you and Alice doing?"

"If my plan works out, very well."

"You're going to propose, aren't you?"

"Yes."

"What are you doing here, then?"

"I'm not meeting her until five."

"That's a poor excuse. When I proposed to my wife I couldn't keep still. I almost asked her over the phone."

"I had that issue last night when I scheduled our date. It is a good thing that I couldn't see her face last night because I practically hung up on her."

"What are you doing here?"

"Trying to keep my mind at ease and my nerves down."

"Well, I've got news for you, then."

"What's that?"

"If you don't get out of here, you are going to be fired. I don't want to see your face until tomorrow morning."

"Fine. I'll go home."

The chief turned and looked out the window to the parking lot. It didn't look like I could fool him.

I turned on my heels and walked to my car. When I was getting in, I waved and everybody who followed me got a weird look on their faces. Especially the other person at the top of the gossip mill, Naomi.

After watching two hours of television, I went to the kitchen and made lunch. I'd never been so excited for anything, and five o'clock couldn't come fast enough.

The girls got home from school and went to their room to do their homework. They were both excited about going to spend time with Casey and Cobalt.

About four thirty, the girls showed up in the living room and asked if we could go. Since I was as excited as they were, we left.

When we got to the ranch, Alice was trying to get up on a new horse, one that she rescued two weeks ago. In the other round pen, Casey was teaching Cobalt how to ride. The girls ran over to them to cheer on Cobalt, and I walked over to watch Alice. Instead of swinging her leg over, she laid in the saddle. When the horse turned, she saw me. She jumped off, and the horse ran to the other fence. "Sorry, I didn't realize how late it was getting."

"That's okay. I'm early."

"Are you ready to go? Mom said she would watch Cobalt."

"She called and asked for the girls too. Let's go." Alice started heading for the car. "Honey, where are you going? We're taking Sarge and Dakota. Casey saddled them earlier."

Alice spun on her heels and walked over to me.

She grabbed my hand and said, "Since I don't know where we are going, you lead." I pulled her into the barn and helped her up on Sarge. I jumped on Dakota, and we went in a dead run toward the fair grounds.

When we stopped she asked, "Why are we here?"

"We are having a picnic in your favorite spot."

"Really?"

"Really." She took off in a dead run toward our destination. She immediately went to the basket.

"Keith, this is so fun." I went and sat by her and started pulling out our dinner. "How was work?" she asked after we started eating.

"Interesting. I got kicked out for the day."

"Why did you get kicked out for the day? What did you do?"

"The boys found a picture of me kissing you and went a little berserk. Chief didn't want me playing twenty questions today, so he told me to go home or I was fired."

"That was nice of him."

"Alice, that wasn't the only reason. There is something I have to ask you." She sat there and waited for me to continue. I pulled out the red velvet case and laid it between us. She gasped as she figured out what I was going to ask her. "Alice, I love you, and that will never change. The girls love you to death. They need a mother who would love them, and you are the best person for that. I see how you are with kids and how much you love Cobalt. Alice, I love you and want to spend the rest of my life with you. I would love Cobalt like he was my own and be the best father to our children. I would be a good son-in-law to Casey." There were tears streaming down her face. I softly wiped them away.

"Keith, I love you, and I know you would be the best husband. You would make a great father to Cobalt, and I would try to be the best mother I could be to the girls. I would love nothing more than to say yes."

I interrupted her. "Then say yes. Why won't you?"

"Because if I say yes, then all the paparazzi will come around and—"

I interrupted her again. "Is that what you're worried about? That when the paparazzi come around, I'll get scared off?" She nodded. "Honey, the paparazzi will not scare me off. I'm more worried what the squad is going to do. I love you. Will you please marry me?"

She nodded and gave me a hug.

"Do I get a kiss to seal that?"

She gave me a kiss, and I said, "I'm glad you agreed, because your mom would have been very disappointed, and so would my boss."

"Can we go home so I can call Rebecca and rub it in her face?"

"Do you want another thing to rub in her face?"

"Yeah."

"Show me the secret passage to get in here." We ran outside and she showed me the passage.

"It's not that secret, but if you don't turn at the right time, you will never see it. Can we go home now?"

"Sure, but you can tell your mom what you decided."

"I think she'll know when she sees us."

"Am I allowed to put this ring on your finger?" I slowly opened the box.

When she saw the two diamonds, she gasped and nodded.

I picked the ring out of the box and slid it on her finger.

We got up and started riding back, side by side and hand in hand.

Chapter 23

Four months later...

Naomi, Rebecca, Mom, the girls, and I went to get our hair done. We had our nails done yesterday. The grown-ups got fake nails and the girls got theirs painted with hearts.

When our hair was done we headed for the church. When I was about to put my dress on, my phone rang. "Hello?"

"Hey, honey."

"What's up?"

"Are the girls behaving themselves?"

"Yes. You better hurry up, or you're going to have to talk to three other women."

"Do I have to show up for the wedding, or can we run to Vegas and get hitched?"

"Sorry, babe. You have to be there. If we elope, my mom will kill us, and your mom would too."

"Fine. See you in two hours."

"That seems like forever."

"I know. Hey!" he yelled at somebody else.

Somebody on the other line said, "You know I could make your fiancée disappear very quickly if you don't get off this phone."

"Noah, if you lay one finger on him, you will have to deal with me and the kids."

"Fine. I won't touch him." He clicked the phone shut before I could say anything else.

Mom finally got me and the girls in our dresses an hour later. Rebecca and Naomi were in their purple bridesmaids dresses and the girls were in their white flower girl dresses. My dress was a white halter top with beads running down the front and back.

We were all standing there waiting for the song to switch when Jane ran over to me. "What's wrong, honey?"

"I have to go to the bathroom." Mom quickly grabbed her and they ran for the bathroom.

When the song switched over they were not back yet. Rebecca held me back away from the door while Naomi stepped in. She closed the door behind her, but I still heard her say, "Please hold tight for a minute. Jane had to go to the bathroom." Everybody chuckled. Naomi stepped back through the doors right as Mom and Jane joined us again.

They opened the doors and walked through. Mom held me back so nobody could see me yet. When everybody was in place, the song changed and I started walking down the aisle. All I could see was Keith.

When it was time to say the binding words, I was crying. Mine came out slurred and very quiet, but Keith's came out loud and clear. Then the preacher finally said, "I now pronounce you husband and wife. You may kiss the bride."

We both fell into each other and kissed. When we pulled apart, Keith said, "Finally. I thought it would never come."

"Me too," I whispered.

When we stepped outside, a million cameras snapped pictures. To give them a good show, Keith leaned me back and kissed me.

We made it to the reception an hour later. The reception was at the barn. When it was time to give speeches, Noah, one of Keith's groomsmen, stood up. He started everything and said, "Before I give my speech, I would like Rebecca, the maid of honor, to stand up." When Rebecca stood up, Noah walked over and knelt in front of her. "Rebecca, the love of my life, will you marry me?"

"It's about time you asked her. I've been pushing you two together from the first time you laid eyes on each other," I said.

"Yes!" Rebecca shouted. Noah stood up and kissed her. Everybody started clapping. After everyone said their speech, Keith and I had our first dance. After a few dances we said good-byes and headed for our honeymoon.

Epilogue

Two years later...

It is our second anniversary today, and Mom is planning this big party. When I opened my eyes there was a big bouquet of roses in front of my face. I smiled and kissed my husband. "Happy anniversary," he said.

"Happy second anniversary. These are beautiful."

"Not as beautiful as you."

"You are so sweet. Now would you like yours?"

"You didn't have to get me anything."

"I didn't get you anything." My eyes shot to my stomach and so did my hands. "I'm pregnant!"

"You're pregnant!"

We didn't get to say more because the girls and Cobalt came running in.

"Happy anniversary, Mommy and Daddy," they said in unison.

"Thank you," I said with tears running down my face. We all got ready and started down the stairs. As we descended everybody clapped.

Rebecca and Noah were married four months after us. They were holding hands and Rebecca was staring at her stomach with a loving hand resting on it. *She can't be pregnant, can she?* I wondered.

When I got a free minute, I grabbed Rebecca and went somewhere quiet. "Are you pregnant?"

"Yes, how did you know?"

"I saw you staring at your stomach and resting a loving hand on it. I did the same thing this morning."

"You're pregnant?"

"Yes." We quickly ran back to the party and were greeted by Keith's parents.

"Alice, we're leaving. Do you have something to tell us?"

I looked over at Keith and he nodded.

"I'm pregnant!" I yelled.

"I'm pregnant too!" Rebecca yelled.

"I'm engaged," somebody yelled from the back of the group. Everybody turned to see who it was. Rebecca and I screamed when we saw it was Naomi. Rebecca and I started running to give her a hug and she hid behind James. James didn't protect her very long because Keith and Noah followed us and were running at James. Naomi and James finally got engaged.

Mom yelled, "Pregnant women aren't supposed to run." We stopped, and instead of us running to her, she ran to us and we passed hugs out.

As the party died down, the old wedding party went inside to talk. The only ones who didn't were Mom and the kids.